THIS IS
ROCK 'N' ROLL NOVEL
EVER WRITTEN...

THIS IS JOHNNY ANGELO, BOOK ONE!

Born in 1946, Nik Cohn grew up on the west coast of Ireland and moved to England when he was fifteen. He is a widely published author whose speciality is books on rock'n'roll. Cohn has had two international best-selling titles, AWOPBOPALOOBOP ALOPBAMBOOM (Rock From the Beginning) and ROCK DREAMS (with artist Guy Peelaert). His other books include MARKET and ARFUR, TEENAGE PINBALL QUEEN, which inspired the rock opera 'Tommy' His latest book is the highly ambitious KING DEATH. Cohn currently lives in New York, where he works as a music journalist on 'The New York Times'

NIK COHN

I AM STILL THE GREATEST SAYS JOHNNY ANGELO

BOOK ONE!

SAVOY BOOKS

In association with

NEW ENGLISH LIBRARY
TIMES MIRROR

This Savoy paperback follows the text of the original
Martin Secker & Warburg edition

Copyright Nik Cohn © 1967, 1980

Cover art and book design: David Britton

Illustration p.1: John Mottershead

Published by Savoy Books Ltd,
279 Deansgate, Manchester M3 4EW,
England

Printed by S.E.T. Limited, Manchester, England

ISBN 0 86130 060 2

PUBLISHER'S DEDICATION

For

Larry Williams)1956-1959) who was a prime mover in the history of rock'n'roll. Who cut the best rock'n'roll records ever made. Who's strange life and bizarre death in Hollywood on 10th January, 1980, leaves so much unsaid.

"Even in decline, he was a smooth man. He wore rings on all his fingers and brushed his hair forward like the Beatles. He had shiny silk suits and ever present shades. And he talked a lot, with a turn of phrase that was truly elegant. In this style, he made my all-time favourite remark about rock: " 'I'm truth,' he said. 'It has no beginning and no end for it is the very pulse of life itself.' " His personality epitomised everything flash and catching about Mister Rock'n'roll." —Nik Cohn, 1965

PART ONE
IN THE ROCK 'N' ROLL LEGEND
OF JOHNNY ANGELO

1 The First Word

Johnny Angelo was a hero. From the moment he was born until the time of his death, he lived the life of a hero, and that was all he really cared about.

Being a hero, he became a pop singer. If he had lived at another time, he might have been a soldier, a politician, a prize-fighter. But Johnny Angelo lived from 1942 to 1966, and he went into pop. It was the only life in which he could achieve what he wanted so fast, so thoroughly and in such style.

This is not a realistic story about the pop business, and it is not an exposé. It is a legend, the legend of Johnny Angelo, the story of what he was and what he dreamed he was, told as Johnny himself might have told it.

2 The Wall

At the age of four Johnny Angelo was a lady-killer.

He had a red suit, a bright red suit. It had tight red trousers that tapered gently to the ankle, and a baggily-cut jacket, low-hung to below the waist, which was given added style by the bulky shoulder-padding. Attached was a matching red hood and, on top of the hood, there was a brilliant white pompom. Again, the whiteness of the pompom was echoed by a white scarf, twirled once, twirled twice around his neck and then slung casually over his left shoulder to trail halfway down his back. Johnny Angelo was a bobby-dazzler.

At the far end of Mrs Angelo's back yard there was a high red-brick wall, ten foot ten inches high by thirty foot long with a thickness of nine inches across the top. It was a weather-beaten and crumbling wall. One day Johnny Angelo did a cat-walk on the top of it.

He climbed the wall in his red suit. He climbed it by centi-metres and millimetres, inching up and falling back again, crawling up it by finger-tips and toe-holds. Twice he fell back to the bottom again; on the third attempt, he climbed it. His head appeared over the top, the shrewd fat face of a baby, puckered with concentration and framed by the big red hood with the white pompom on the top.

His mother was hanging out washing in the yard below, sheets and blankets that were caught by the wind and billowed up into her face. It was a very windy day, fresh and cold and sunny; a day for earmuffs and fried breakfasts, early in March. The wind blew grit into Johnny Angelo's face, but he went on hauling himself up the wall inch by inch, pulling himself up by the strength of his shoulders until first his left knee then his right knee was solidly on the top. Then he stood up and dusted himself down. He brushed the dirt and moss off his kneecaps and he flicked the long hair out of his eyes.

He looked around. He'd never been so high in his life. His mother was struggling with a yellow bath towel in the yard

below. His mother was a grey, haggard woman, thirty-eight
years of age, and the towel picked her up and waltzed her
across the yard, backing and advancing, swinging her around,
holding her, stroking her. Her hair came loose from its pins
and trailed down into her eyes and got into her mouth. She
stumbled against a broken bucket and almost fell.

Johnny Angelo shot her down with his forefinger. Then he
did the catwalk. His knees were stiff and his back was straight,
his head was held high, his eyes looked straight ahead. He
kept his bottom tucked in, his chest well thrown out. His red
suit shone.

He was marching in the style of the Nazis. His red suit was a
uniform. He marched from one end of the wall to the other,
and then back again. He marched stiffly, the leg perfectly stiff
at knee and hip. He looked magnificent. His scarf billowed
behind him in the wind.

Mrs Canning from 23 was the first to see him. She was
washing her windows and she saw him on the wall, a baby
aged four, fat and squat and very solemn, his white scarf
behind him in the wind. She threw up her window and
screamed.

"Johnny! Johnny! Come down off that wall! Are you mad?"

Johnny Angelo kept marching, stoutly, methodically, in a
perfect rhythm.

The black cat from next door sensed trouble, ran for cover.
The birds stopped singing, the dogs ran away with their tails
between their legs. Mrs Angelo stopped dancing with the
yellow towel. "Come down off that wall!" she shouted, "come
down, Johnny, before you do yourself an injury!"

Johnny took no notice. He turned at the end of the wall and
began the slow march back, stiff legs and arms and the red
suit shining. Windows flew up all along the street, heads hung
down, women were screaming, their hair in curlers. Come
down, Johnny, come down; come down this very instant or
you'll catch hell. Johnny didn't. It was a beautiful, sunny day.
He marched from end to end of the wall in his bright red suit.
Once his foot slipped, a brick broke from the wall and fell and
split in two, the wall began to crumble. Mrs Angelo screamed.
Johnny Angelo kept marching. Mrs Angelo was beginning to
have hysterics. Johnny was tiny on top of that great wall, and
he had a long, long way to fall. His mother let the yellow towel
flutter from her hands and drop to the ground. Mrs Canning

was crying for the fire-engine.

Mr Gunter from 34 came down in his shirt-sleeves and began to climb the wall. He was a very big man, a heavy man with a big beer belly; climbing didn't come easily to him. Once, twice, three times he slipped, barking his shins, scraping his kneecaps, bruising his elbows; but still he clenched his teeth and climbed. His breath was coming fast and heavy, his eyes were gleaming red. "It's all right, Johnny," he said. "It's all right. I'm here. I'm here."

Johnny Angelo paused to flick dust from his cuff, to adjust the flow of his fleecy white scarf; then he went on marching.

"Hold on," said Mr Gunter. "Just hold on, Johnny, I've got you."

Johnny stopped and looked around him. The whole street was watching, the whole block, the whole neighbourhood. Mr Gunter was crawling on all fours along the top of the wall towards him. Johnny Angelo set off marching to meet him. The wind whipped them; the sun shone on them; the wall trembled as they moved. Mr Gunter was scared. He looked down into the yard and felt dizzy. "Hold on, Johnny," he said again, cooing. "I'm coming. I'm coming as fast as I can."

When they had got within two yards of each other Johnny Angelo stopped and stared at Mr Gunter. "Come on, Johnny," said Mr Gunter. "Come to me, come to your Uncle Gunter." He made a grab for Johnny Angelo, and missed. Johnny didn't move. Mr Gunter inched forward and made ready to lunge again. No one moved, no one made a sound.

Suddenly Johnny laughed.

He laughed quite calmly, a gurgle, a goo. He swung his legs over the side of the wall, shinned down it in one, two, three long swings and tumbled into the waiting arms of his mother.

"Oh Johnny, Johnny," she said. "You naughty, naughty boy." And her tears fell down and soaked his face, as she carried him into the house.

While in the back yard Mr Gunter was still crouching on the wall.

3 The Back Room

At the age of six Johnny Angelo was a mother-hater.

Mrs Angelo wore a white quilted nylon housecoat that was stained to grey and brown. It was frayed at the hem and worn almost through at the elbow. She wore it slouching in the kitchen, reading the papers. She was wearing it in the morning when Johnny Angelo went out to school and she was still wearing it when he came home in the late afternoon.

She smoked cigarettes from the corner of her mouth, smoking them down to the filter tip without touching them, and the ash fell off onto the carpet. She wore her thin hair up in curlers and dyed it blonde out of a bottle, and the dye ran into streaks and patches. Her hair was blotchy. Her skin was blotchy, too. Johnny Angelo thought his mother was a slut.

She let her home fall into disrepair. There was a front room and a back room, an attic upstairs, and the back yard. The back room was the kitchen and the washroom and the dining-room. The front room was the living-room. His mother slept on a wide couch in the front room. Johnny Angelo and his two sisters slept in three fold-up beds stretched end to end along the walls of the back room.

She let the brown paint peel off the back room walls and did nothing to put it right. Johnny Angelo was ashamed to come home from school. The beds weren't made, dirty washing was stacked in the sink, the drains smelt bad. There was a sad sick smell everywhere.

She sent him to school in socks that didn't match, and she let his black hair grow long until it fell forward over his eyes; and she slashed it with the kitchen scissors holding his head over the sink. She tried to make him go on wearing his red suit when it was all gone through in the knee and the hood had been torn off in a fight; she wanted him to go on wearing his beautiful red suit with the big hood and the white pompom till it hung off him in rags. But Johnny Angelo put his foot down, his red suit was sacred. One boiling day in August, he took it to the bomb site and buried it.

He had two sisters he hated. The thing he hated most was menstruation. He hated the sight of bloody towels in the back room. He shrank from the sour smells in the sheets. His sister Ruth had hysterics every month, the day before she came on. she screamed, threw books, spat. Johnny Angelo went for a long walk to let it pass. The house was filled with the feel of blood and sickness.

He was a solitary. At the age of six, he didn't want his mother's black bras lying on his bed, he didn't want filthy windows and unwashed dishes and men he'd never seen in his life before coming out of his mother's bed in the mornings. He was fastidious. He hated squalor and bickering.

He was never a child. He never cried, he never got excited. At the age of seven he was a heart-throb. His black hair fell forward over his eyes in a rakish cowlick. His white teeth sparkled after brushing. He had deep black eyes.

He wanted his daddy but his daddy wasn't there. His daddy had run away when Johnny Angelo was born.

The back room was dark and dirty and smelt of yesterday's warmed-over stew. Johnny Angelo was sent to bed at seven, directly after he'd finished his tea. Motor bikes were revving up in the street outside. His sisters were playing dominoes on the table. His eyes were opening and shutting. His mother was sitting by the fire with her eyes closed. The fire was on her face; fire and shadow, noise and silence. He folded his knees into his belly and composed himself for sleep.

He woke again at half past ten. No one was moving. The room was quiet. He was hot and thirsty and restless, and he wanted a drink of water. Also, he was afraid of the dark. He wanted his daddy.

There was a light still on in the front room. He could see the light sneaking through the crack in the door. He got out of his bed and tiptoed.

His mother was with a man. The man was fat and pink and wore a pair of tattered white underpants, his belly sagging heavily over the top. His mother was lying stretched out on the couch. She had no clothes on. She was very thin.

The window was open, it was stormy outside. The light bulb was swinging in the draught. The man lay down beside his mother and began stroking her arms and breasts and belly. He rolled over on top of her. Johnny Angelo could hardly see her,

crushed beneath him. The wavering light rushed over them
and ran away, ebbed and flowed, flooded them again; it hurt
his eyes to watch. The man was biting his mother's ear.
Johnny Angelo went back to his bed and did nothing. He just
remembered it, that's all.

Or when his sister Ruth brought home her boy friend Ron,
and he caught them on the back room couch. They had their
clothes on but his hand had disappeared in the depths of her
skirt and his face was red, deep red or purple, the colour of
beetroot. Johnny Angelo stood and watched them. He didn't
laugh, didn't cry, didn't shout or stamp. Just snickered. Tee
hee, like that, snickered. And for a long time, too, snickered
and snickered until they stopped.

His mother sent him to school when he was five. He sat in
the third row, handsome Johnny Angelo, making paper pellets
and dipping them in ink and flicking them at the boys up front.
His teacher was gangling and spotty, about thirty. Johnny
Angelo thought he was cissy. He liked to scream and storm
and come on strong but Johnny had his measure right away.
The teacher asked Johnny how much was five times five.
Johnny said that five fives were twenty-five.

"Five fives are twenty-five SIR," said the teacher.

"That's right," said Johnny Angelo, "twenty-five."

"Twenty-five SIR."

"Twenty-five."

"SIR."

"Twenty-five," said Johnny Angelo.

He had a uniform again. His blazer was a deep wine colour
with a yellow dragon on the breast pocket. His cap matched,
and it had a strong yellow band; and his socks were grey, with
wine and yellow stripes.

He was solitary. He was arrogant. He stood in an empty
corner of the playground and when the bell went he was
always the last to troop back into the classroom.

"You're late," said the teacher.

"Yes," he said.

"Sir," said the teacher.

"Yes," he said.

He refused to undress in public. At the age of six he was
expected to play football, he was meant to change with the
other boys. He went into the changing-rooms but wouldn't
take his pants down. When the other boys were running out in

their brand-new shirts and silver studding, Johnny Angelo
stayed behind. The teacher came in and looked at him.

"Angelo," he said, "get changed."

"No."

"Get changed," he said, "this instant. I command it." His
face was yellow with rage and malice.

Johnny Angelo sat sullen and half naked on the bench, and
shook his head.

The teacher stepped forward to hit him, then backed away.
"Get changed," he said.

"No."

"Why not?"

Johnny Angelo just sat and shook his head. He sat and
looked at the teacher, and the teacher looked back. Stalemate.
The teacher stood with his hands on his womanish hips and
looked at Johnny Angelo, and Johnny Angelo sat on the bench
and looked back at the teacher. The teacher tried again. "Get
changed," he said.

"No."

"Get changed!"

"No."

"Call me sir!" said the teacher, "damn you, call me sir, you
little bastard, you little shit! Don't look at me that way, don't
try to come it with me, you little shit, don't you dare! And
CALL ME SIR!"

"SIR," said Johnny Angelo, "sir sir sir sir sir, sir sir sir,"
till the teacher plugged his ears.

"Stop it," he said.

"Yes, sir."

"Get changed."

"No, sir."

"Why not?"

Because he wouldn't take his pants down. Because he was
ashamed. Because he had made up his mind. And when
Johnny Angelo made up his mind he never changed it.

4 The Attic

At the age of seven Johnny Angelo was a jackdaw.

His mother was forty-one years of age. She was poor; she had to take in washing and she had to scrub floors. She had to have lovers who left her presents. Johnny Angelo caught flies in the front room.

His mother was thin and tired and grey-faced. She coughed in the mornings, and gasped for breath and stopped to hold her side halfway up a flight of stairs. Johnny Angelo didn't like her; she smelt of tiredness and boredom. She was dumb and drawn and ill. Johnny was bored with living in dark rooms, bored with unpainted walls and yesterday's potatoes. He didn't like sleeping in the same room as his sisters.

He wanted his daddy.

His mother woke up coughing in the mornings. He heard her scuffle in the front room, groping for her slippers, coughing and gasping and wheezing, grunting like an old sow. She came through into the back room, her hands out before her for support and her hair falling in rat's tails to her neck, her skin grey, the dirt black beneath her finger-nails. She reached for a cigarette; her hands were trembling, she fumbled with the match, the cigarette shook between her lips. She turned her blank face towards him. The tap was running. The milkman knocked on the door. Johnny Angelo rolled over. Turned his face to the wall.

The same people, the same faces, the same expressions, day after day. The same walls, the same bad drains, the same third-hand, crumbling furniture. Johnny Angelo was bored.

He was sent to bed at seven.

His sisters played card games on the back room table, straining their eyes in the bad light. His mother was talking to a man in the next room; the door was closed and light was coming through the cracks.

He lay in his bed, pretending to be asleep, but his eyes were open, he was watching.

"Johnny, go to sleep."

"Johnny, I'll tell your mother on you."

"Johnny, I'll tell on you."

No talking; SLAP, a card hits the table.

Silence. The silence builds, and SLAP, another card hits, breaks the silence. Then the silence clamps down again, this time it lasts for five seconds: SLAP, another card. The two girls look at each other across the table: SLAP, another card. Then a silence of ten seconds: SLAP. Waiting in silence SLAP in the bad light SLAP waiting for the cards to fall SLAP SLAP SLAP.

"Johnny Angelo, I can see you."

"I'll tell on you."

"I know you're watching."

"I'll tell your mother on you."

"Ooh Johnny, I'll tell."

"Ooh Johnny."

He watched through half-shut eyes. His mother laughed in the next room. The cards slapped on the table and he wasn't allowed to watch.

At the age of seven Johnny Angelo decided he had to get away.

There was an attic upstairs. Dirty, dank and damp, ten foot by seven. The roof slanted in from a maximum five foot three to a minimum two foot nine. The attic was filled with discards, with thrown-out clothes and bedsteads and moth-eaten carpets. Rain came through the roof; the wind broke off bricks and tiles from the wall outside. The skylight rattled in its frame. Johnny Angelo sat cross-legged on the floor. It smelt of ratshit and mothballs, rain and dust and cold. It was his personal property.

He stuck a sign on the trapdoor, white paint on cardboard: Private property, keep off, trespassers will be prosecuted so stay away. Keep off. Signed, Johnny Angelo.

He climbed up to the attic by a rope ladder, and drew the ladder up behind him. He drilled a peephole in the trapdoor and squatted for hours on the attic floor, his eyes to the hole, watching.

It was cold in the attic. It was harsh and smelly. It was raw and uncomfortable.

He spent whole weekends locked up on his own. He was a solitary, a brooder. He watched what was happening through the peephole. He saw the men who came to visit, he saw his sisters playing cards on the kitchen table. He watched the cards slap down. He heard his sisters singing out of tune.

His mother shouted for him to come down. "Come down!" she shouted. "Come down, your dinner's ready! It's on the table, it's getting cold. Come down this minute, you little brat; come down before I make you!" She shouted and swore until she choked and collapsed in a fit of coughing. But Johnny stayed in the attic.

He sat and sat, hour after hour, cross-legged on the floor. It was an October night, it was dark outside, the rain was drumming on the skylight. Rats were chattering in the floorboards. There was a smell of boiling cabbage, wafting up from the back room. He picked his nose. The feel of dust and ratshit clogged his nostrils.

He was a jackdaw.

He stole anything he could lay his hands on and hoarded it in the attic. Books, caps, turnip watches. He wasn't greedy or sentimental. He didn't want anything valuable. He simply wanted everything. Everything. He stole water pistols and diamond rings. He wanted to turn his attic into a treasure house, he wanted to fill it from wall to wall with booty. He stole books, shirts, football boots, nuts, bolts, spanners, toy cars, comics, watches, big turnip watches, badges, popcorn, school caps. Sorted and catalogued and stored: a dumdum thirty-eight, a cowboy hat, a handkerchief, a hundred bang-bang caps, a Spaceman Dan Dare mask, a gun. He filed, stocked. Gloated on them in the privacy of his own attic.

He specialised in turnip watches—big fat turnips with umpteen hands. You open them up and it's like dissecting a frog, there's so much to notice, so much to study and compare, it makes your head spin, hands that turn fast and hands that turn slowly, the ticking of engines and motors and tiny cog-wheels that interweave, that twine and part again, over and over, the endless complexity of it, it's like a brand new cosmic system. And then the front, close it up again, the front is so fat and smooth and smug, those strong black lines on the white face, the fatness of it, it's a comfortable thing, a turnip, to jingle in your hand when you walk to school, to look at under the desk, to keep as a pet.

He took twenty of his best turnip watches and took them to pieces. Spread out the bits in front of him like a jigsaw puzzle

on the attic floor, springs and wheels, a hundred different
shapes and sizes laid out before him, and he studied them.
And from all these watches he wanted to create one new one, a
model of his own design, a turnip that had never been made in
the history of the world.

He sat cross-legged on the cold hard floor and worked. It
grew dark outside. At half past nine, his mother called up to
him. "What the hell are you up to now?"

"I'm making a watch," said Johnny Angelo.

"And Jesus Christ," she said, "haven't you already got
enough watches to do a nation; haven't you got enough
watches up there to keep us all awake in our beds with the
ticking?"

"I want to make a watch of my own."

"For Jesus Christ," she said. "That boy, that boy."

He made the watch. It had five hands and they all went
round at different speeds. They didn't keep anybody's time on
earth but Johnny Angelo's. He created his own time cycle, 34
hours a day, or 29 or 19, or 12, or 8½, a total of five clocks to
be chosen according to his mood. But within their own terms
they never missed a trick, they ran as smoothly as butter in the
frying-pan. And if anyone asked him for the time, he told him
half past five or twenty-two minutes past ten or eighteen
minutes to three, he told him exactly what he felt like telling
him; he chose his clock at will.

And then the other thing about turnips, they were wonderful
to steal. Round and smooth and sleek and warm, they nestled
like pink mice in the palm of his hand.

He went thieving.

He was a pretty boy. He was eight years of age, tall for his
age, well made. He had long black hair that fell forward in a
cowlick over his eyes, and his eyes were big and black and
beautiful. Old gentlemen adored him.

He went thieving in the Sunday morning markets, where the
pickings were easy. Fruit markets and flower markets and fish
markets. Where the crowds were packed elbow to elbow,
swearing, shoving, sweating, getting nowhere; and juicy
turnip watches winked at him everywhere he turned, sat snug
in the warmth of their pockets. Winked at him and said Come
and get me. They might as well have presented themselves to
him on a silver salver. His long lean fingers reached out and
hooked them one by one. He never missed.

He was a showman. He was a big ham actor. He wandered alone and forlorn in the streets of the Sunday morning markets, no one to hold his hand, no one to look after him, poor Johnny Angelo. At eight years of age he was an orphan, cast out into the jungle of the markets and he was pushed, he was bullied, sometimes he was knocked over. Ignored and maltreated by everyone, he walked alone in the main alley of the bird market, there was no one to protect him. Tears came to his eyes.

Winkles, eels, cockles, whelks. Hot pies, hot pies. Canaries and mockingbirds and nightingales. Fresh rolls. Yards of yellow silk. And noise all around him. Great beery men who shouted in his ear. Fat women who trod on him. Shouting and shoving everywhere. He stood and stared and the tears ran down his cheeks.

Lost. Abandoned.

And then, the man. About sixty years of age, discreet, well mannered. Dressed in a grey suit and grey velvet waistcoat. With a fresh red carnation in his buttonhole, and a silver turnip in his fob.

"Are you lost?" he asked. Sonny, he called him. "Are you lost, sonny?"

"Mummy, mummy," said Johnny Angelo. "I want my mummy, I want my mummy. I've lost my mummy and I want her back."

"Poor laddie," said the man. "Poor lost laddie."

Another tear trembled on the brink, was tenderly brushed away by a silk handkerchief. And Johnny was consoled, petted, coddled. He was promised his mummy back. He was bought candyfloss. There was a protective arm round his shoulder. He tried to smile; he tried hard to smile through the blur of his tears. His bright white sharpened teeth showed through and his hands crossed over, another turnip slipped smoothly into his sleeve.

He ran away. He dived into the market and disappeared. Under his arm there was a small black Gladstone bag. The watches jingled in the bag as he ran.

He had a big mirror in his attic, four foot two by two foot eight, rimmed by an ornate gilt frame. He set it up against the slanting roof, jamming it between the ceiling and the floor. And he studied himself.

He posed. He picked up a golden turnip with silver engrav-

ings, and he held it out in his left hand. He smiled, he
frowned, he winked. He picked up a plain silver heavy turnip
with a false compartment for photographs at the back and a
sepia snapshot of a gentleman with fine curly moustaches and
an eyeglass and he put it in his breast pocket so that the
winder peeped coyly out over the top. He made faces. He put
his two thumbs into the corners of his mouth, his two fore-
fingers in the corners of his eyes. Or he had a navy blue school
cap, one of his favourites, and he pushed it forward on his
head so that it covered his eyes, and he blew out his cheeks. Or
he thumbed his nose.

He looked soulful. Turned down his lips and drooped his
nostrils, oozed soul. Or sat cross-legged and watched himself.
Sat and stared. Sat with his back to the mirror and couldn't
resist sneaking a sly look at himself over his shoulder. His
mother was shouting for tea. He liked the way he looked.

The food was burnt. The back room was filled with the smell
of burning. Thick smoke choked him when he opened the door.
The windows were steamed up. His mother and his two sisters
were sitting at the table. Johnny was given the chair with one
leg too short, and the plate that didn't match. The eggs were
stuck to the bottom of the pan and came out torn and black and
hard. His sister Ruth had long greasy hair that fell forward as
she ate and trailed in her plate. She never looked where she
was eating. She collected egg and grease on the end of her hair
until it hung off her like candle grease. She had a big grey wet
snot on the tip of her nose; it hung and trembled, it hung, it
finally dropped off and fell into her plate.

Somebody farted.

His sister Candy was talking with her mouth full. Johnny
Angelo was thinking of his attic and the mirror. He was thinking of the way he looked.

"Don't bolt your food," his mother said. "You'll give yourself bellyache."

"Say something when I speak to you," she said.

"Something," said Johnny Angelo.

"Sauce," his mother said, taking no notice.

She was worried about him. He was obstinate and sullen
and solitary. He took all kinds of airs on himself. His mother
thought he might be stealing. He thought that everybody was
plotting against him.

"Sauce," she said. "Now eat your tea."

She was a thin, sick woman, too tired to cope with him. She ran her hand through his hair. "Sauce," she said. But she was thinking of something else.

Somebody farted again.

After tea he went back to his attic. He arranged five of his biggest and best turnip watches in a row in front of the mirror, and sat down cross-legged behind them. It made a very beautiful composition.

He sat and stared. Himself and a row of five watches. He sat watching for a very long time. It was dark outside and he didn't get up to switch on the light. He could hardly see. But he sat and watched. And even when he couldn't see at all, when it was completely dark, he was still sitting on the floor and staring straight ahead. Thinking of the picture and thinking of his reflection. Thinking of the way he looked.

He needed to trap it, he needed to get it down in black and white. To have it as a record.

He went out to steal a camera. At four o'clock in the morning he hurled a brick through a shop window and listened to the crash. No one came. He reached his hand through the hole and picked out the biggest camera in the shop. He liked doing it. He enjoyed in particular the sound of falling glass. And he walked all the way home with the camera tucked openly under his arm, straight down the middle of the empty High Street.

At dawn, he took pictures of himself in the mirror, pictures of himself squatting behind his row of five turnip watches, pictures of himself smiling and pictures of himself looking sad.

Pictures of Johnny Angelo.

5 The Cards

Johnny Angelo was a bad loser.

He played three-handed whist with his sisters, one half-penny a game, in the long summer evenings, crouching over the bare and scratched back room table, the fading sun trailing through the window and halfway across the floor. Chewing gum the three of them. Tense and grim, slapping down their cards without talking; Johnny Angelo wouldn't even allow himself to smile when he won. And he won all the time.

He had little piles of halfpennies arranged neatly in front of him, three tidy piles. His tie was slewed round halfway down his chest.

They hated him. They sat facing each other across the table, the two sisters, signalling to each other, winking, nodding, constructing traps for him. He slid out of them without even seeming to notice them. He shuffled his cards in one fast blur like the professionals in the films. He dealt without moving his hands. He was smooth and arrogant, a cool operator.

His mother was in the front room, being laid. They could hear whispering and scuffling, and the creaking of the springs of the couch. Johnny Angelo pulled in the cards. "Let's quit," he said.

"No."

"Not yet."

They couldn't quit. They couldn't let him get away with it. They had to beat him. They had to grind him down.

He shuffled the cards with one hand, unwrapped fresh gum with the other. He half smiled to himself and wriggled his shoulders. He threw down his cards without looking at them. He played one-handed and curled his lip at every card they played. They had to beat him.

He won. Won again. He was winning all the time.

His mother was whimpering in the next room. The sun was shrinking back against the wall. It was ten past seven and he was still winning.

"Let's quit," he said.

"Not yet."

"Chicken," his sister Candy said. "Chicken. Don't try to chicken out."

He wasn't fussed. They went on playing and Johnny Angelo went on winning. The pile of halfpennies got bigger and bigger in front of him, and his sisters were grey-faced, red-eyed. Mean, mean, they wouldn't let it go. Had to beat him once, they said. Had to wipe him out.

The cards slapped down on the table. The table was scratched and chipped, pitted, ravaged and it wobbled on one leg. The sun went in and it began to get dark and he went on winning. He was bored stiff, but still they wouldn't let him stop. Had to beat him just once, they said. He could hear his mother making love again next door.

Then he got careless. They set him up, he wasn't watching, and they ran him through. He lost and had to pay out four halfpennies. Four halfpennies out of forty-two and he was on his feet, shaking.

"Cheat," he said. "You cheated me."

On his feet, hissing, his face clenched tight and his two arms dangling useless down his sides: cheat, cheat. Cheated me. Set me up. Made a monkey out of me. Hissing at first, choking, then screaming: cheat, cheat, cheat.

The two sisters held out two halfpennies each and spun them in turn. Faces fat and smug as butter, they looked at him; not laughing at him, not looking sorry, not looking anything. Empty faces: beat you, beat you, we beat you, we beat you rotten. Beat you.

He had lost. They set him up. They planned it, waited, calculated, laid traps. They had cheated him while he was off his guard. They had deceived him—sly, slimy, underhand, evil. He faced them, lifted the table and overturned it. Cheat, he was screaming, cheat, cheat, lousy stinking cheat. The halfpennies exploded on the floor.

Silence. The noises in the next room had stopped.

Halfpennies rolled underneath their feet and the sisters didn't shift. The table collapsed between them and they looked at Johnny Angelo: beat you, we beat you. No let-outs, we beat you. He wanted to strangle them. He stared at them, but there was nothing he could do. His face swelled and he turned away. Cheats, deceivers. Two-timers, betrayers. He ran out of the

house. Ran out crying into the street and was ashamed to come
home.

Cheated, cheated. All around him, people were plotting,
were deceiving him and planning his downfall. Behind his
back. Over his shoulder. Plotting and planning.

At school, in morning assembly boys were pointing dirty
fingers at him, whispering about him behind their prayer
books. Nudging and giggling. He knelt to pray with his head
down, eyes clamped shut. The headmaster was up on the
rostrum, making a speech, standing on the rostrum in a black
gown. Terrible words, Johnny Angelo didn't understand
them. Terrible words about himself, words that fell into the
hall like ugly black bats. And the headmaster was pointing at
him with a long bony forefinger; he was shouting, shouting at
Johnny Angelo, this black headmaster ten feet tall. Johnny
Angelo knelt to pray. He shut his eyes and didn't dare to look.
There was a scuffling and a whispering behind him, giggles
and hysterical choked-off laughter. They rose to sing, to chant
the morning hymn. The headmaster was going to call his
name, Johnny Angelo, Johnny Angelo, come out, come
forward, stand out before the school. Johnny Angelo, dis-
graced, humiliated.

They sang hymns but nothing happened. No one called his
name. The headmaster was coming down off the rostrum and
nothing happened. They were trooping back to their class-
rooms and no one had said a word to him. He was safe. It was
all over.

But he still heard the sniggering behind his back, the scuffling and the laughter only just held in control. It was louder
now, it billowed up behind him, open and arrogant. He turned
to face them and they were laughing behind their hands at
him, red fat bloated faces, sly deceivers' faces, hideous faces,
they were laughing themselves sick, pinching themselves,
reeling, laughing. Laughing at what? At nothing. At him.

And in the classroom the same thing. There were the same
hands moving on the desks behind him, the same hands pointing, the same hands passing messages.

"What's so funny?" demanded the teacher. "What are you
laughing at?"

"Nothing."

In five minutes it had started again, a steady murmur of
laughter at his back, and out of the corner of his eye Johnny

caught glimpses of the same faces, red laughing faces that
followed him everywhere.

"What's so funny?" said the teacher. "Tell me what it is."
He was angry this time. He went down to the back of the class
and picked on the smallest boy he could find.

"What is it?" he said. "Why are you laughing? What's so
funny?"

"Nothing," said the boy. The teacher picked him up by his
neck and slapped him. "What's so funny?" he repeated.
"You little creep, what are you laughing at?"

"Angelo," whispered the boy. "Johnny Angelo."

Johnny Angelo was on his feet and tearing at his back. In his
hands a crumpled, tattered bit of paper. On the white paper in
big black letters, three inches high, KICK ME SAYS JOHNNY
ANGELO.

Kick me.

Kick me. The class was in an uproar. Johnny Angelo stood
staring at the paper while the class roared, jeered, kick me,
kick me. The teacher was laughing too. Kick me, kick me,
KICK ME SAYS JOHNNY ANGELO. He looked up and everyone was laughing.

Laughing at him. At Johnny Angelo.

There was nothing he could do but stand there and look at
the paper in his hands. Kick me says Johnny Angelo.

In the swimming-pool they sneaked up behind him, smelly
cold fingers over his eyes, and ducked him till he choked. They
dived in on top of him, crushed him, or splashed him with
water, threw water in his eyes until the chlorine turned them
red and blinded him. In the changing-rooms they caught him
and took his pants down, holding him down when he struggled, punching him, bruising him; they took his pants and
wouldn't give them back. He was made to stand with his pants
off and told to beg to be given them back. But he wouldn't beg.
He stood and waited. They dangled his pants in front of him
like bait; he wouldn't rise. They threw them down on the floor
in front of him; he wouldn't bend to pick them up.

They got tired of it. They threw the pants into the swimming-pool and left them to float, jeering at him, catcalling. But
he wouldn't make a move to fish them out. He waited. They
got bored with him and went home. One round to Johnny
Angelo.

He was a solitary. He needed to be brought down. Stuck-up,

snot-nosed Johnny Angelo.

He had inky pellets flicked at him in class. Dead toads were left in his desk. Ink was spilled on his homework. His books were scrawled over or stolen. His locker had obscenities carved deep into the wood: KICK ME SAYS JOHNNY ANGELO.

Prettyboy.

Prettyboy Johnny Angelo, too big for his boots.

Johnny Angelo the biggest arsehole.

The way he sat alone in his corner of the class. The way the girls adored him. Prettyboy Johnny Angelo. The way he never talked. The way he curled his lip. And now the way he wouldn't bend, wouldn't shift an inch: they hated him. It wasn't dislike; it was real hate. Why? Because he was a solitary? Not quite. Because he was arrogant? Not just that. Because he curled his lip?

Because he was Johnny Angelo, that's all. Because he was Johnny Angelo.

Hated by the boys, worshipped by the girls. Prettyboy Johnny Angelo.

Going home from school, they were waiting for him. Round every next corner, down every back alley. Catcalling, throwing stones, waiting to beat him up. Sneaking up behind him or waiting in ambush ahead of him. Swarming all around him, planning, plotting, cheating, deceiving. He wouldn't give in to them, he wouldn't go home a different way, he wouldn't run, he wouldn't even walk faster. Mule-headed, he wouldn't let them see him bend.

They got tired of waiting. They didn't throw stones and they didn't beat him up any more. And Johnny Angelo survived.

But was it quite like that? Was it that bad? Johnny Angelo said Yes, it was.

And don't all boys get bullied? And don't all boys get KICK ME written on their backs? And don't all boys get their pants pulled down in the changing-rooms? Not like me, said Johnny Angelo, I was different. They hated me.

Hated him? Why?

Because he was Johnny Angelo.

6 The Gunfighter

Johnny Angelo was a gunslinger.

From the time of his birth he lived the life of a hero. That is at the heart of everything; everything can be explained by that. Johnny Angelo could not bear to live the life cut out for him. He lived the life of a gunslinger.

On his eighth birthday, he got the full gear of a gunfighter. It was cheap imitation and tinsel but serviceable and it was the best he was likely to get. High-heeled black leather boots with silver spurs and glass studding down the front; long lean leather pants, tight at the ankle, slung low on his hips; white dude shirt with a lace-frilled ruff running down the breast; three-quarter-length classic gunfighter's black coat; pearl-handled six-shooter, Billy the Kid model, in his glass-studded black belt; black leather gloves, tight, and black stetson. With it came a pack of cards and five hundred caps for the gun. The total cost was seven pounds nineteen and eleven.

Johnny the Dude. He had to pawn his watches to buy it. He went down to the pawnshop loaded with twenty-seven turnip watches, and plumped them down on the counter. His whole collection gone in one minute. His collection that had taken him one year and a half to build, he traded it in for a gunfighter's uniform. And he had meant to hand in his own watch, too, the watch with five hands; but at the last second he pulled it out of the bag and put it away in his fob pocket. Because he needed it to tell the time.

It was his eighth birthday, and it was the hottest day of the year. No one moved. People sat on doorsteps and sweated, or huddled in pubs and drank cold beer to keep sane. It was a Western day, the kind of dry dusty unbearable day they're meant to have in Reno and Dodge City and down the O.K. Corral, when the gunfighter rides into town. When dogs go mad and the sun hurts your eyes. When everyone is too dry and burnt to speak. When the car tops are so hot it burns your fingers to touch them. No one worked. The schoolgirls mean-

dered back through the town and dust climbed up their legs.
The boys came by on bicycles and stopped to chat them up;
they bought the girls ice-cool lollies at the corner stand, and
maybe stole a kiss in the ice cream parlour when no one was
looking and the juke box was playing something sentimental
like Kisses Sweeter Than Wine. That kind of a day.

Johnny Angelo was standing outside the toy shop in his new
uniform. He stood on the kerb and looked around. His thumbs
were hooked through his gun-belt and his feet were planted
well apart. He was up on his toes, sharp and ready. Looking up
and down the street. It was his first uniform since he buried
his red suit on the bomb site.

He was a gunslinger, moody and magnificent. He peered
out from under his stetson, staring up into the noonday sun.
He spun his six-shooter in his hand, chewed gum, looked
mean. They he started walking down the sidewalk, walking a
nice slow easy roll, pigeon-toed, a gunman's strut, and all the
time his hands were hovering just above his holster. His
trigger finger itched.

Look out. Look out. Johnny Angelo's in town.

The sun burnt down. Sweat started to run down his forehead
and into his eyes. His white frilled shirt was clinging to his
back. His scalp itched under his stetson and he couldn't get
used to the four-inch heels; he kept lurching off the pavement
and into the gutter. Everyone turned to stare at him. As he
came round a corner the whole street would stop dead. People
would pause just where they were and watch him, follow him
down the street and out of sight. Johnny Angelo moved slow
and easy, kept his eyes wide open and his body tense. For
danger. People were stirring in the shadows behind him, or
over his shoulder, watching him, waiting ... or spied on him
from behind curtains. Or someone in an upstairs room was
planning his destruction, someone who wouldn't come out in
the open. Into the street. Where Johnny Angelo was as watch-
ful as a long lean cat.

Black stetson and long black gambler's coat and high-heeled
black boots. He was eight years old. He was three foot eleven
inches tall.

The sun. Johnny Angelo went on walking through the heat.
People watched him, mesmerised. Life had stopped. No one
moved. Johnny Angelo drifted down the middle of the street
like a night rider through a ghost town, like a flying Dutch-

man. Through the slow salty heat; men stopped and straightened as they worked, or froze as they were getting into their cars, one foot still on the pavement. Women put down their shopping-baskets. Johnny Angelo slid through them, a gunslinger walking through waxworks. He never flicked an eyelid, he never wavered. He went walking, easy, easy, and his head never turned to left or right. As if he didn't know he was being watched, as if he didn't even realise there were people all around him. As if he was sleepwalking.

But inside his uniform, under the black coat, his body was exploding. He was melting in the heat; sweat was gushing down his back in rivers, running into his eyes until he couldn't see, making him feel faint. His head was humming, his brain was buzzing. He thought he was going to fall down. He couldn't afford to do that, he would have lost his cool. And he couldn't do that, at all costs he had to keep his cool.

Keep your cool, that was his favourite phrase, you have to keep your cool. Lose your cool, he said, and you're dead. Even when you're fainting and the heat is burning through your back, your head reeling and a whole street watching you, staring at you and waiting for you to go wrong—you can't afford to bend. Stay cool, stay sharp, stay hard. Flunk out, he said, and you're done. At all costs keep your cool.

In the shadows behind his back something moved. A dog scratching itself. Johnny Angelo whirled in one movement, and his gun was coming out of the holster as he turned, up to his hip, and bang, bang, bang, three shots blasted out one after another, the noise like an earthquake in the street. The dog ran. Johnny Angelo was left on the sidewalk, his six-shooter smoking in his hand, the black leather glove as sausage-tight as a second skin. It has to be said, he looked silly.

Some hipster he was at the age of eight. Johnny Angelo, gunning down dogs in the open street.

It was a little girl aged about six, in blue jeans and a tight sweater, who was the first to laugh. She sat on the kerb with her feet in the gutter, and she pointed at Johnny Angelo and laughed. Her laugh was high pitched and it carried as clear as a bell. Johnny Angelo took no notice. He went on walking, the same easy lope and sway, the same pose of the hands just above his gunbelt. Johnny Angelo did not deign to recognise the existence of six-year-old girls in sexy sweaters who laughed at him.

Too late: the spell was broken, the magic cracked as he walked. "Gunslinger!" shouted the girl. "Walking like you had crabs in your pants!"

"Cowboy!"

"Gunman!"

"Look out, gunman, Jesse James is on your trail!"

Laughing at him, pointing, jeering. The whole street unfroze in ten seconds, melted with every step he took. He looked around him; there were laughing faces everywhere. Leering faces behind the net curtains. Behind closed doors, smirking. Fingers pointed at him. The schoolgirls and their lovers were standing at the ice cream stand and they shouted at him as he passed: Gunslinger, gunslinger.

He backed away. There was red in his eyes; they hurt, and he couldn't see straight. His heel caught in a crack in the pavement and he nearly fell. He put up his black-gloved hand to shield his eyes. Against the faces.

Faces that jeered, that smirked and sneered at him. Great smelly mouths, stuffed with onions, that breathed in his eyes and roared. Red faces, great bloated red beer faces, drunken, crude, that dripped sweat like candle grease. Shiny faces, shapeless faces. Faces that howled and bayed for blood. Faces of cruelty and greed and drunkenness. That crowded in around him, that surrounded him and wouldn't let him out. And he backed away until his back was up against a wall, until he was trapped, and he could see only blurs of faces in front of him, green faces and red faces, red faces and purple faces. Dissolving faces that still laughed at him. Crowds all around him, laughing. Like the kids in school who wouldn't let him be, who hounded him and wrote KICK ME on his back. Who persecuted him and drove him halfway mad. Only this time there were more of them and he was more exposed. And it was hotter; the heat blazed down on them, on him and on all of them. And every sound was multiplied, every face was three faces. Johnny Angelo, backing away, shrinking, hiding himself, was faced by an army. Five thousand onto one. Onto him.

Johnny Angelo was concerned. His back was up against the wall. He was stuck in his corner like a rat and he thought he was going to cry.

"Gunslinger!" screamed the girl in the tight sweater.

"Cheyenne!"

"Lone Ranger!"

"Greasy Mex! Greasy Mex!"

Johnny Angelo was down on one knee, by the wall, blazing from the hip, shooting from his left hand and fanning with his right. He shot wildly into the crowd, bang, bang, bang, blind and mad and crying. He couldn't see where he was firing; he just aimed it low and let it go. He backed away again and started to run, covering himself as he ran, shooting over his shoulder or even half-turning in his stride, bang, bang, bang, bang. He ran; and no one followed him. He stopped to look back. They were fifty yards away, but he could still hear them laughing. He stood on the horizon and wiped his eyes. Then methodically he took aim, and one by one he gunned them down, sighting each one in turn, setting himself steady and firing; he gunned them down until there wasn't one left standing. He didn't stop shooting till he ran clean out of bang-bang caps.

He was thirsty.

He felt flat the way all gunfighters feel flat when the shooting has to stop.

Gunslinger. He wiped his gun-barrel. He wiped the sweat off his streaming hands and squatting in the road reloaded his six-shooter. There was no one in sight. He was alone. The sun blazed down upon him. He pulled his stetson low down on his forehead and straightened up his Mississippi string tie that had gone askew in the gunfight. His throat was dry and crusty. He was dying of thirst.

He squinted into the sun, not knowing what to do, not even knowing where he was. He felt that he couldn't breathe and his eyes were hurting even with his stetson pulled down low. The sun burnt down on him and he was lost in some streets he didn't know, grim little slum streets. Streets as dry and bare as the Arizona desert.

He went on walking. Stetson and six-shooter and black dude coat. Housewives stared at him from behind their curtains and didn't dare to come out. And didn't dare to laugh at him. A sinister figure to walk through their back yards, a gun-slinging dwarf in a long black coat and stetson. Sweat and dust slabbed on his face like pancake make-up and he was limping badly because he wasn't used to high-heeled boots. His spurs were clattering against the cobbles.

He came out into a wasteground, walking very slowly,

dragging his bad leg painfully behind him. And dust rose up at every step and settled on his coat.

The wasteground was a bomb site or perhaps a stretch of common land too rough to be turned into grass. Pitted and ridged it was, sprinkled with coarse patches of grass and weed but made up mostly of parched mud that had split into great cracks with the heat. Scattered with bricks and broken glass, tin cans and the abandoned bodies of old cars. Brass bedsteads and suitcases, orange boxes, old furniture, skeletons of rusty bicycles.

It stretched for perhaps three hundred yards and on the far side of it there was a children's playground, and in the playground (even Johnny Angelo could see) there was a giant drinking-fountain. Water, ice-cold water. And Johnny Angelo was dying of thirst.

Three hundred yards to go. And he was fainting with the heat, his leg was throbbing and his head was going to burst. And on the other side there was water waiting for him, as much cold water as he could drink. On the other side of the desert. He started to walk towards the fountain.

The ground was deeply pitted underneath his feet. At first he stumbled on every step he took. His knees would buckle and he would nearly fall. He would trip on the broken handlebars of a bicycle or he would bark his shins on a camouflaged tin can. Hard going. Slow graft. His leg was aching, his heels were blistered raw and bleeding. And he couldn't keep his balance on four-inch heels, or walk straight in long-point shoes that pinched his toes. Agony. He walked for five minutes and looked up at the drinking-fountain. It was still three hundred yards away.

But he went on walking, reeling and staggering like a Chicago drunk, and the sun belted straight down on the back of his head, grinding him down, frizzling him until his brain went round and round, and he couldn't see where he was going. He had to sit down. He sat down on the sharp point of a broken bottle. His black coat was creased and dusty. His brand-new tight black leather gloves were scuffed across the knuckle. Sitting down, the heat was even more blistering than when he was on the move. And he started to walk again. He wasn't thinking straight any more. He thought he was maybe ten yards away from water, and then the next moment it was ten miles. He thought he was lying down; then he thought he was dying. He dreamed he was drinking in the water. And the sun was turning his head. Or driving him crazy like happens to dogs. He wasn't walking right, he was weaving round in slow circles. And he tripped in a rat hole and fell forward, flat on his face. Put his hands out to protect him and landed on broken glass, that ripped through his leather gloves and tore his hands. He knelt in the wasteground and blood was soaking through his gloves, oozing out and dripping onto the ground. He looked up and the sun was shining straight into his eyes.

Eight years old. Three foot eleven inches high. In a long black dusty dude coat and torn gloves, white frill shirt and Mississippi string tie. And crucifying high-heeled shoes. Gorgeous Johnny Angelo, now fallen on hard times. But he hauled himself back up on his blistered feet and walked towards the fountain. No one could call him gutless. Johnny Angelo, no one could ever say he wasn't determined.

And he wasn't going to let three hundred yards of wasteland get him down. He wanted a drink of water. He could see the fountain. And he walked towards it.

Also he wanted to be a hero. If he couldn't be the new gunman in town, he could be a rancher crawling on hands and knees across the Arizona desert, while the sun burnt him to a crisp.

He was shrinking. Housewives hung out of their windows watching him, and the further he walked the smaller he got. He was standing in the middle of the wasteground, looking up at the sun. He was moving forward. He fell over. He got up again and started walking. He was tiny at that distance, a tin soldier walking round in circles. The sun must have been driving him mad; he was getting confused and walking the wrong way. Or he stepped into a pothole and half of him disappeared. But re-emerged again, filthy, tattered, and started walking. Moved forward. And the sun played tricks with him and led him round in circles. But still he was moving forward.

Johnny Angelo wore a black coat and a stetson and black gloves and high boots with spurs. And a white shirt and a Mississippi tie and an ornate gun-belt that glittered, shimmered in the sun. He was wearing a brand-new uniform but it had taken him only one afternoon to ruin it.

He was lost in the middle of the wasteground. He was

staggering round in circles. The sun burnt down until he fell onto his knees and started crawling.

All because he had to be a hero.

7 The Cat

At the age of nine Johnny Angelo was a fly catcher.

He was all alone in the house. His sisters were at school and his mother was out shopping. It was eleven o'clock in the morning. Johnny Angelo stood at the front room window.

Of all the rooms in the house he hated the front room the worst. On the mantelpiece there was a photograph in a gilded frame of his father. His father was wearing a white collar and discreetly striped tie and his toothbrush moustache was newly trimmed. He was smiling vacantly into the camera. His eyes were nervous. He looked nice.

His mother's bed wasn't made. Johnny Angelo was fastidious, and if there was one thing he hated it was the sight of rumpled sheets and pyjamas thrown just any old way on the pillow. And the smell of stale mother that filled the room.

He looked at the photograph and thought how much he wanted his daddy.

So he caught flies. He hid behind the curtains and waited for them to buzz. He stood with eyes tight shut, listening for the buzz of flies. Heard one, a buzz, high up on the ceiling, droning east and downwards towards the window. He was poised, a big whte napkin in his hand. And the buzzing dropped in past his left ear, zzzz, getting louder, ZZZZ, then it spluttered out against the windowpane. He opened his eyes: pig-eyes, set deep in the sockets. Cold shrewd pig-eyes. The fly was crawling on the window. It looked contented. Johnny Angelo raised his napkin and took aim, waited a second, then brought it down lightly on the crawling fly. A quick flash of white in the grey room, and the fly dropped stunned but otherwise unharmed to the floor. It lay there without moving.

Johnny Angelo picked it up and carried it to the table, and he laid it out carefully in front of him, taking care not to bruise it. From the time of his birth Johnny Angelo had always been by nature a perfectionist.

He picked up the fly by one of its wings and the wing came away in his fingers and the body of the fly flopped back onto the table. He picked it up by its other wing and again the wing came away, again the body fell back onto the table. The fly was kicking its legs and trying to escape but it could no longer move.

Johnny Angelo was very careful when it came to detaching the legs. He wanted to do it cleanly and without mauling the body more than necessary. But in time he had taken off all the legs and the fly was left on the table to die. It took a long time to die. Johnny Angelo kept prodding it with a matchstick and if it moved that meant that it was still alive. Finally, he poked it and it didn't move. And he knew that it was dead.

He put the dead fly in a tin box and in that tin box there were already dozens of other dead flies.

Johnny Angelo was collecting. When he had collected exactly fifty flies, no more no less, he went out one afternoon into the bird market and bought a beautiful green and yellow budgerigar. He brought the budgie home and kept it in his attic, where he looked after it lovingly and fed it well and fattened it up until it was as plump and healthy as a budgie could possibly be. He taught it to speak. He would go up to the attic every morning before he went to school and as soon as he opened the trapdoor the budgie would swing on its bar and preen itself and say: JOHNNY ANGELO JOHNNY ANGELO JOHNNY ANGELO. And every time the budgie got it right, Johnny would give it a reward, which was one of the dead and by now rotting flies. And the budgie accepted the dead flies willingly and one by one he gobbled them up until there were no more flies in Johnny Angelo's tin box.

Then Johnny Angelo went round to the bomb site one morning and collected a boxful of small, sharp stones. It was cold and muddy and stones were hard to come by, but at the end of an hour he had all the stones he wanted and he took them back into his attic.

The budgie was sitting in its cage at one end of the attic floor. JOHNNY ANGELO, it said when it saw him, JOHNNY ANGELO JOHNNY ANGELO. Johnny sat down at the far end of the attic and began to shoot off his stones at the captive budgie from a peashooter.

Trapped in its cage, the budgie tried frantically to escape, clawing at the bars and screaming. Johnny Angelo shot it down. The stones twanged out of the shooter and smashed into the bird's feathers, bruising, gouging, drawing blood. It took a long time. For a full hour Johnny Angelo sat at the far end of the dark attic and fired off stones at his budgie. There was a litter of bloodied stones on the floor of the cage. The budgie was weakened, exhausted; it stopped trying even to get out, but just crouched on the floor, blind in one eye, and let the stones thump home into its body. At last it fell on its side, its legs up in the air, though it still struggled to get back on its feet, and Johnny Angelo closed in and let go a quick hard volley into its unprotected belly. JOHNNY ANGELO JOHNNY ANGELO said the bird and fluttered its wings. It lay still on the floor of its cage, huddled into a corner. Blood came from its beak. Then it was dead.

Johnny Angelo stored the dead bird for safety in his school luncheon box, then went out into the animal market, and bought himself a cat. It was a beautiful, fat, black cat, sleek and smug. It had a sly contented look in its eye. It had a purr of sheer evil. The kind of cat, if you looked closely enough, you could see was a nasty bit of work.

He carried it through the open streets, his big black cat purring in his arms. From time to time he patted it on the head. Man and beast, they knew each other well. They knew just what they were up against.

The cat was given the dead budgie and it ate it, purring between each mouthful. The cat sat in the attic and the sun came through the skylight. The cat lay down and toasted itself. Its belly was full of good meat and rumbled with contentment.

Johnny Angelo watched the cat and smiled, the way a father does when he looks at his baby.

Johnny Angelo and his black cat. They were inseparable. They went to school together in the mornings, Johnny Angelo leading, the black cat following, and the cat sat on the grey school wall, in rain or in sun, and waited through the day until his master came out again and walked him home. Or the cat stole for him. Sneaked into the High Street store and brought him out long strips of liquorice with lemon sherbet in the middle, or socks that came up past the knee and were striped

in red, white and blue, or even ties with drawings of Dan Dare
on them. A smart cat, sharp dealer, it stood in the High Street
and licked itself, looking innocent. Policemen stopped on their
beat to stroke it. And the cat and Johnny Angelo looked at
each other, saw themselves reflected in each other's eyes, and
smiled. They understood each other well.

Johnny Angelo's mother never liked the cat. The cat used to
pussyfoot around behind her. Sometimes, when she had a
hangover or she was doing the washing up, the cat would
creep up behind her and very gently rub its tail across the back
of her legs. It scared her out of her mind.

The cat sat on the rug in front of the fire. Purring, licking
itself, looking so sweet. But its eyes were gleaming and it
never stopped smiling.

Angelo and the cat. They had the same eyes. Great black
eyes that glowed in the dark. And they tiptoed round the house
together, smiling.

His sisters hated Johnny Angelo and hated his black cat.
They hated the way they were so smug, so superior all the
time. They thought it was time for Johnny Angelo to come into
his come-uppance.

One day when Johnny Angelo was out and his cat was lying
in the sun in the attic, the two sisters gave it poison in its
saucer of milk. Angelo came home to find his black cat dying.
Writhing on the floor and thrashing about with its tail and
screaming in agony. There was nothing for him to do but sit
and watch it die.

He could be very proud, Johnny Angelo. He wasn't going to
break down. He knew his sisters were waiting for it, and he
wasn't going to cry. He sat at the table and watched his beautiful cat twitch until it died.

And then his cat was dead. His black cat with the big black
eyes that were always smiling. The cat that ate the bird that
ate the flies that ate the germs on Johnny Angelo's windowpane.

PART TWO
IN THE ROCK 'N' ROLL LEGEND
OF JOHNNY ANGELO

8 The School

This is Johnny Angelo in his teens. No little boy now, no more childish tricks. This is Johnny Angelo when he was already a climber.

When he was fourteen he was big and handsome, with a great cowlick of black hair down in his eyes and a loose walk. And then, his eyes... big, sad, black eyes, deep as black eyes could be. Pretty eyes and evil eyes. Or signifying eyes.

Signifying sex. Johnny Angelo at fourteen was a sex symbol.

He walked to school in the morning and all the little girls of the Remove, the Fourth and Fifth, plus a few cradle-snatchers of the Lower Sixth, hung low from their classroom windows and watched him. Hung out of the window with their green skirts rucked up way above the knee and their pigtails swinging, waiting.

They waited a long time. Johnny Angelo made a point of coming in late; he liked to lay on a little agony. And the girls hung low and waited for him. The bells were ringing for morning assembly, the prefects were trying to shift them and the teachers were standing on their dignity but the girls wouldn't shift until they saw him; they dug their heels in and wouldn't budge an inch. Johnny Angelo kept the whole school waiting.

He came round the corner, smiling faintly to himself. His back was loose and his arms were swinging at his sides, and his secret eyes were masked by the black blur of his hair.

Someone screamed.

He was carrying his books under his right arm, tied up in red braces, he passed the school windows, staring straight ahead. And then just when he was nearly past, and the girls were hanging out of the windows, sighing and begging in their hearts for just one glance from him, he did—he half turned, half looked, half smiled. He let a little flicker of a smile flicker into one corner of his mouth. And he let his hand half trail behind him, extending it to the girls.

Another scream. And another. And another. Heart-throb Johnny Angelo. Even at the age of fourteen he was a show-man.

The boys didn't like it. Johnny Angelo walked to school and all the girls would start to scream. The boys didn't like it one bit. They thought he was a pretty boy, the way he smiled and all those sly glances he used, and his fluttering eyelashes, coming on sexy like he was the new Elvis Presley. They thought he was a nance. It isn't decent, is what they thought. Johnny Angelo is a Cissy Boy, they said. Johnny Angelo is a Cissy Boy.

It was resentment, that was all; at first it was just a mild case of jealousy. But the more the girls loved him, the more the boys didn't. After three months Johnny Angelo began to find notes in his desk.

> Johnny Angelo Get Your Hair Cut.
> Johnny Angelo Who The Hell Do You Think You Are?
> Fairy Johnny Angelo.

When Johnny Angelo walked to school, his hair fell forward black and shiny in his eyes. He wore scarlet shirts open at the neck, and white shoes with golden buckles. His hair was long and shining. He had sideboards past his earlobes and his hair curled up at the front in a heavy quiff. His sexy smile went all lopsided. And the girls screamed for him.

On the blackboard he found his name written in great white letters.

> Johnny Angelo We're Watching You.
> Johnny Angelo You Floppy Prick.
> Johnny Angelo.

On his chair there were sharp tin-tacks which made holes in his shiny black-and-gold-striped pants. In his desk, there were toads, dead or alive.

What did he do? He did nothing, of course; he ignored it. He refused to take any notice. He looked in the mirror and combed his hair.

It was taking shape already: Johnny Angelo, loved by the girls, hated by the boys.

He had an ally, whose name was Catsmeat. Catsmeat was

six months younger than anyone else in the class, and his ambition in life was to be a slave to Johnny Angelo.

Catsmeat was what is known as mentally deficient. Fat and white and puffy, like pastry. White-skinned and albino, his fat face shapeless and featureless. He sported an American-style crew-cut.

At the age of four Catsmeat was ignored by everyone; he was a leper. At the age of six people began to take notice. They teased him and hit him and threw stones at him, called him names and stole from him. And he liked it; it was at least attention of some sort. Then at the age of ten the bullying stopped. He was ignored again. He was on his own. Other boys were embarrassed by him.

Then he fell in love with Johnny Angelo.

In the gymnasium, he stopped and sucked his thumb, paralysed by the beauty and grace of Johnny Angelo. In football, when Johnny Angelo was downed, he turned his head away and couldn't bear to look. And at the end of his Geometry test, when the master came round to collect his paper, his page was blank but his blotter was cluttered with tiny drawings of Johnny Angelo. The master was angry with him and Catsmeat cried.

Catsmeat was ugly and stupid. On his fat fingers he wore silver rings, three on each hand, and on his feet he wore bright yellow socks which glowed in the dark. But he loved Johnny Angelo.

At the end of each class he would get up quickly and run to the door and wait there for Johnny Angelo, and when he came Catsmeat would jump forward, tripping over his own feet, and open the door for him. Angelo swept through without a look or a word.

Johnny Angelo didn't dislike Catsmeat, or despise him. He never noticed him.

Johnny Angelo was a solitary. He was cold and aloof and untouchable. He made no friends and he was suspicious of everyone. He carried a looking-glass on him and combed his hair during morning prayers. And he was hated.

He was hated by all the boys. He was hated because he was handsome and all the girls were crazy for him, and because he loved himself so much. The boys wrote slogans about him on the blackboard.

Johnny Angelo You Nothing Bum.
Johnny Angelo The Greatest Crud.
Johnny Angelo Try Sucking Your Own Cock.
Johnny Angelo The Shit.

But Catsmeat thought Johnny Angelo was the most beautiful man in all the world. He was in love with him. He prayed
for him and to him at night. He longed to kiss his feet.

After school the boys waited for Johnny Angelo. They stood
at the corner of an alley and waited for him to come by. It was a
burning hot afternoon. Johnny Angelo was wearing his light-
weight purple summer blazer with the emblazoned silver
dragon, and he was smoking a cool cigarette out of the corner
of his mouth (look, no hands) and he was doing this kind of a
walk called Shooting the Agate. He put his two thumbs into his
belt and hunched his shoulders; he flicked his ankles out sideways at each step and kept his feet well apart and pigeon-toed;
of all the young boys in town who tried to shoot the agate, no
one could do it as well as Angelo. He seemed to skim the pavement in one continuous revolving movement, as if he were
wearing skates. And the boys in the alley were waiting for
him.

It was really very hot, so hot that it was claustrophobic. It
was probably as hot as that day years before when Johnny
Angelo went walking as a gunman.

Catsmeat was following, ten yards behind, his walk half a
trot and half a drunken stumble, his trousers tight to bursting
across the rump, his white face dripping sweat. He wanted to
speak to Angelo, but he couldn't pluck up the courage.

The heat was bouncing off the pavement. On each side of
the street the houses were of red brick, the kind of red brick
that crowds in on you and chokes you, and the heat was
trapped by them and doubled and then trebled. The heat
bounced back and forward between the houses and Catsmeat
was being grilled alive. Johnny Angelo felt the heat but he was
not in the habit of sweating.

"Johnny," called Catsmeat. "Can I walk with you?"

"Huh?"

"Johnny, Johnny Angelo. Can I walk with you? Can I? Do
you mind if I walk with you?"

Angelo didn't say No and he didn't say Yes; he just walked
straight on without even looking round. Catsmeat shambled

behind him, one step back, lagging, one yard behind, falling
back to two yards, and three yards, and then putting in a little
agitated spurt to catch up again, running, trotting, falling over
behind Johnny Angelo.

"It's hot," he said, "isn't it?"

"Huh?"

"I said it's hot."

"Yeh."

It was. It was boiling. Steam was rising off the pavement.
Catsmeat was suffering.

"Slow down," he said, "let's take it slower. Let's take it
easy." And round the next corner the boys were waiting. It
was all red brick and burning rubber and car tops too hot to
touch. Catsmeat's feet were swelling up inside his shoes and
his shirt was rubbing red and raw against the back of his neck.
Sweat was dripping into his eyes so that he couldn't see. It was
the hottest day of the year. Of any year.

Red brick could be very heavy and there were hundreds of
tons of it all around them, pressing in on them and squashing
them. The street was like a cauldron.

The boys were waiting at the corner. Eight of them, squint-
ing into the sun. Their shirts were open and their ties were
slewed round under their ears. Their arms were hanging low
at their sides, and they had peeled back their cuffs and rolled
up their shirt-sleeves past the elbow.

They could see Johnny Angelo coming but he didn't seem to
be moving, his legs were working but he wasn't coming any
nearer. In heat like that, nothing moves. Everything hangs.

Johnny Angelo was walking more slowly and Catsmeat was
dragging behind him.

"Johnny," said Catsmeat, "don't go on. Stop here. Don't
go any further."

"Sod off," said Johnny Angelo. "You creep. You little runt.
Why don't you sod the hell off?"

Catsmeat dropped back, lagging five yards behind. They
were both walking on, but now they were moving very slowly.

"Don't go on," said Catsmeat, "they're waiting for you.
They're waiting to beat you up."

"Who's they?" asked Johnny Angelo.

"I don't know."

"Why are they waiting? For me?"

Catsmeat blinked. It was hard to think in such heat.

"I don't know," he said.

He was telling the truth. He didn't know, he really didn't. But he guessed and he was sure of it. He could see round corners, and he knew the boys were waiting.

"Why should I stop?" demanded Johnny Angelo.

"I don't know."

"Why?"

Johnny Angelo shook his head; his black hair tossed back off his forehead and then fell forwards into place again. He thought that Catsmeat was a cretin. He walked on.

"I don't know," repeated Catsmeat. He was panicking, his voice had gone high and shrill, and he was running along behind Johnny Angelo, pleading with him.

"Stop," he begged, "stop, stop, please stop." Sweat was dripping off his face and splashing onto the pavement; his fat legs were bursting out of his trousers.

"Go away," said Johnny Angelo.

But Catsmeat refused to give up. He sweated and he whined and he pleaded, stop, he said, please stop, and even though they were moving very slowly and it was a boiling day, the corner of the alley was right ahead of them, twenty yards ahead, then fifteen, then ten. And round the corner the boys were waiting with their mouths open and their fists up, avengers, and the red-brick houses were red-hot all around, and the street was full of burning rubber. And Johnny Angelo didn't stop.

"Go away," he said again.

Catsmeat hesitated for only one moment and then did the only thing he could possibly do. He ran ahead and plunged round the corner ahead of Johnny Angelo. The eight boys pounced on him and swallowed him up. Angelo stood back and watched and Catsmeat's white albino face, roasted red, turned back towards him. Triumphant.

Johnny Angelo turned away.

9 The Weasel

Johnny Angelo was trying to look like Elvis Presley. He grew
his sideboards until they were over four inches long and
threatened to meet under his chin. He stood in front of the full-
length mirror in the attic and practised Presley's lopsided sexy
thick-lipped smile and dazed stare. Or he stood with his feet
apart and made his legs vibrate, from the heel to the knee,
from the knee to the pelvis, at first slowly, one leg at a time,
then faster, then both legs together first slowly and then
faster, until he was shaking like a bowl of soup, the floorboards began creaking, and his mother banged on the ceiling
because her men friends didn't like it. Johnny Angelo was at
this time fifteen years old and he lived for Elvis Presley.

But he still missed his daddy.

He had a picture of his father pinned up on the attic wall, his
father as a young man of twenty-five in baggy pants and an
open shirt, standing awkwardly and grinning, his eyes
screwed up because he was looking into the sun. It was post-
card size, this photo, yellowed and curling at the edges. It
stayed on the wall for many years, then suddenly it began to
look too shabby and he took it down and burnt it.

He could well understand why his father had disappeared so
suddenly. When Johnny Angelo came in from school his
mother would be sitting at the kitchen table, reading the
paper. Her dress was torn, her fingernails were dirty, her
mascara was streaked; she was fifty years old and ugly and
skinny and shapeless, and she didn't have the dignity to let
herself grow old. She slabbed on make-up and she brought
home men. She was lazy and sluttish. She disgusted him.

His father was a tidy man, you could tell that from his photo,
he was clean and fastidious. He wasn't the kind of man who
would or could put up with sluttishness. He was like Johnny
Angelo himself in that respect.

Angelo was spending all his time in the attic, mixing with
his family as little as possible. He disliked intensely the way

their dirt got into his skin and clogged up the pores, the way their smells of washing-up and smoke and sex got in his hair. It was like sullying his brilliantine with diesel oil. He hated it. So he sat by himnself and tried to look like Elvis.

"Why don't you talk to your family?" asked Catsmeat.

"Because they're peasants."

"How peasants?"

"Filthy," said Johnny Angelo. "Filthy."

News came through that his father had died, aged sixty-six, of pneumonia and complications in some flop-house in another town. He hadn't held down a job in two and a half years; he had lice in his hair and there wasn't enough money on him to pay for burial. Johnny Angelo's mother had the body brought home and buried her husband in the local cemetery. She bought flowers for the grave and cried when they let the body down, cried bitterly, digging her nails into her wrists to keep the pain back. But Johnny Angelo, his son, refused to go to the funeral.

He took the photograph in the gilt frame from the front room mantelpiece and broke it over his knee. He tore the photograph itself into small pieces and threw it out in the bomb site, where he'd also discarded his red suit when he was a child.

He wouldn't give any reasons. That bastard, was all he would say, that bloody bastard.

He moved away from home. He rented a small room of his own. It cost him thirty shillings a week.

It wasn't palatial. It was a small damp room with brown wallpaper and a brown carpet. The floorboards creaked with every step he took. It wasn't heated properly, just a paraffin stove, and the electric light fluttered all the time. It was lit by one small dirty window. Johnny Angelo's sensitive stomach turned over every time he walked through the door.

Catsmeat came in twice a week to scrub the floors. He washed Johnny Angelo's dirty underwear and he cleaned the windows. He wore a white apron and carried a feather duster, and he cleaned the room until it was spotless, and when he had completely finished, he began cleaning it again. Johnny Angelo sat in the coffee bar across the street and drank Coca-Cola.

It was a dirty little hole. On bad nights, the rain came oozing through the ceiling and formed a puddle at the foot of the bed. Rain water ran down the inside of the walls and his clothes were always soaked when he got up in the morning. The only heating was a paraffin stove, and even that didn't work properly. The room was usually icy and miserable.

He sat in the coffee bar and watched the traffic. The waitress loved him; she brushed against his back every time she passed, she leant close to him and breathed into his ear and she rubbed her breasts against his shoulder. He got a double helping of froth in his coffee.

About every half an hour or forty minutes or so he would go back to his room. Late one evening he found Catsmeat there, squatting on all fours with his head under the bed, dusting in the corners. There was dust everywhere.

"Well," said Johnny Angelo, "have you finished yet?"

"Nearly," said Catsmeat, "I still have to do the mantelpiece."

"And the window," said Johnny Angelo, "the window. Look at it, it's filthy. Just look at it."

The paraffin heater was wheezing by the window, the room was full of fumes. There was a big photograph of Elvis Presley facing the bed. Catsmeat scrambled to his feet.

"I'm sorry, Johnny," he said, "I'm sorry."

Johnny Angelo and Catsmeat, they went everywhere together. Don Quixote and Sancho Panza.

Johnny Angelo wore black leather to school. He wore a tight leather jacket, a windbreaker that zipped up the front and had silver studding round the pockets and a silver dragon emblazoned on the back; and black jeans as tight as sausage skins and black winklepicker shoes and black tight leather gloves and big black shades to hide his evil eyes.

He was a Teddy boy.

The girls hung out of their windows and screamed; opposite, the boys flung up their windows and jeered and threw stones into the street. Johnny Angelo passed right through the middle, chewing gum, his hands deep in his pockets and his shoulders hunched, shooting the agate. Arrogant Johnny Angelo, who knew how to keep his cool. Hipster Johnny Angelo, loved and hated.

Catsmeat shambled two steps behind him, carrying his schoolbooks. Johnny was lean and elegant. Catsmeat was fat and cretinous. Johnny walked in front, Catsmeat lagged behind. The girls faced the boys, and the boys leered at the girls, high above their heads.

Everywhere Johnny Angelo went, Catsmeat was lagging two steps behind him. Servant and bodyguard. Disciple and chopping-block. He carried Angelo's books to school.

This was the beginning of the Rock era, everything was new and rough. The whole teenage thing was just beginning. New: Rock itself and wild clothes and juke boxes and froth on the top of coffee. Riots and rumbles. A man aged thirty-five walked into the coffee bar one night and tried to play a Vera Lynn record, but the kids wouldn't let him. He stood up and said they were a crowd of hooligans and a good thrashing was the best thing for them, and they beat him up; they put the boot in and drew him out into the street. Later, on his way home, they slashed him with razors. All because he couldn't stand Elvis Presley.

It was a very passionate time, it was one of the most exciting times there's ever been. Johnny Angelo would go to the coffee bar every night, Catsmeat trailing in behind him. They sat in the far corner booth by the juke box, out of the cold, cupping soggy cigarettes in the palm of their hands. The juke box was made of silver and gold, and it had highlights that twinkled and it played fantastic records: Larry Williams, Bony Moronie. Bill Haley, Don't Knock the Rock. Little Richard, Miss Ann. The record Catsmeat loved most of all was Laurie London singing He's Got The Whole World In His Hands. He thought that was beautiful.

The volume stayed switched on way up loud just as long as Johnny Angelo sat there. He didn't want to hear anything in the world but good hard Rock, he didn't even want to know anything else existed. On his back, in great high silver letters, his leather jacket read ELVIS.

Johnny Angelo ruled the roost. He had that coffee bar twirled right round his little finger.

Catsmeat wore black leather and had greasy hair and he carried a flick knife in his breast pocket. Hipsters sitting in the other booths tried to snigger behind his back but Johnny Angelo just had to look at them once and they faded away. No one questioned the authority of Johnny Angelo.

He got his coffee with double froth and he cleaned his nails with a flick knife. No records got played, just the records he wanted to hear.

Before he came out each night he combed his hair for half an hour, staring at himself in a tiny, chipped pocket mirror that stood on his mantelpiece, the electric bulb flitting like a frightened moth on the ceiling.

Catsmeat waited for him outside. He sat on the stairs and waited for Johnny Angelo to come out.

Then they sat in the coffee bar each night from half past six till midnight. Drinking coffee and listening to the juke box. It dominated Johnny Angelo's life, this coffee bar where he was King.

There was a kid called Benny who only came to the coffee bar about once a month maybe. He belonged to a different crowd. One night he came in looking mean, Benny, he went straight up to the juke box and put on a Bill Haley record. Then he turned round and waited to be challenged.

"Elvis Presley is a bum," he said. "Elvis is a screaming nance. Bill Haley is King. Bill Haley for ever."

He was known as the Weasel, because he was skinny and shifty, and he was squint-eyed.

"Fuck off, Weasel," said Johnny Angelo. "Nobody called for you. Run away and hide. Trickle."

"Square," said the Weasel. "Elvis is a bleeding square. And so are you, Johnny Angelo, you're a square too."

Johnny Angelo leant back and took a long cool drag and then laughed. Catsmeat snickered behind him, dutifully.

"Ooze off," said Johnny Angelo. "Ooze right away. Trickle," he said, "you haven't got your balls yet."

It was a ritual: the Weasel pulled out his flick knife, and his squint-eyes went small and black deep down in his face. And Angelo smiled and yawned and pulled his flick, too, the two of them facing each other across the table. Up on tiptoe, circling, feinting. Backing, advancing. And the big black silent circle all around them, closing in, watching, watching. It wasn't any contest. The Weasel dummied and struck and missed, Angelo just took his time and brought his knife down on the Weasel's wrist. The Weasel's flick clattered to the floor and he was standing there with empty hands and blood was pumping out of his wrist in a fountain; he was trying not to cry out in pain and humiliation, but the tears kept escaping. Angelo was right behind him, holding the Weasel's arm up high against his back and pressing it higher.

"Say it," said Angelo. "Say it. Elvis is the King."

"Elvis is a Square."

Johnny Angelo put the hurt on until the Weasel screamed

and everybody held their breath. Catsmeat was laughing so much that it hurt.

"Say it. Say it."

"Bill Haley is the King."

"Say it."

"Bill Haley."

And Angelo grinned and squeezed and twisted just a little more till he could hear the joints begin to crack in the Weasel's arm.

"Say it," said Johnny Angelo.

"Elvis is the King," said the Weasel.

Johnny Angelo let him drop on all fours on the floor, where he writhed and twisted without making a sound. Johnny Angelo was standing over him, smiling, showing off his beautiful gleaming white teeth. Suddenly the coffee bar was full of noise and laughter, and the juke box was playing Blue Suede Shoes by Elvis Presley. The Weasel was crouching on the floor, his face black with pain.

"Do it again," said Catsmeat. "I liked it so much."

10 The King

Elvis Presley was still the King.

A week later they went up to the Scala to see the King's new movie, Elvis Presley in *Jailhouse Rock*. They queued in the cold and driving December rain, their pockets bulging with knives and hammers. Women were staring at them and muttering, hooligans, hooligans, there ought to be a law. Hooligans, they said, it's a disgrace, it's a disgrace.

The Scala was big and cold and high; a vast amphitheatre where the back row was one hundred and ninety feet from the screen and the cinema organ played selections from *Kismet* and there were double seats in the back row. Friday night, it was packed out.

No popcorn tonight, no ice cream, no orange drinks, no nuts and raisins. Male attendants walked the aisles with torches, and the doors and walls were lined with policemen with truncheons. Because troublemaker Elvis Presley had come to town. Kissing lovers were thrown out in the street and all undesirable characters were searched for offensive weapons on entry. But Johnny Angelo smiled his beautiful smile, and no one dared to question him. He sat near the back and Catsmeat sat next to him, and his teeth shone like pearls in the dark.

"Johnny," said Catsmeat. "I want to go to the lavatory."

Jailhouse Rock: Elvis was an orphan who killed a drunk in a fist fight and got himself sent to the penitentiary. In the penitentiary his hair was cut and his sideboards were peeled off. The girls in the audience began to cry. He got mixed up in another fight and was whipped for it; the girls cried some more, and this time Catsmeat was crying, too, his head in his hands, it was all too much for him. But later Elvis became a rock 'n roll singer and swiftly rose to international fame as the heart-throb of millions. Then he went on television in his own show and dressed up in a convict's uniform and sang Jailhouse Rock.

"Johnny," said Catsmeat. "I have to go to the toilet."

Dance to the Jailhouse Rock. Johnny Angelo was slashing up his seat with his flick knife. The stuffing came spilling out in grey and musty handfuls, and he flung it over his shoulder into the row behind. He put his knee through the seat in front of him, the noise of the wood cracking like the world exploding. And the police were stampeding down the aisles with their truncheons flailing, women were screaming in the dark of the back stalls and flick knives were glinting everywhere. Jailhouse Rock: Elvis was dancing, his hips were switching like roller coasters, he was smiling that thick-lipped lopsided smile of his, leering over his shoulder. Sexy and arrogant and magnificent he was; he was wearing a striped convict's uniform and glowering, and his sideboards ran black and shiny down his cheekbones. The girls were screaming Elvis, Elvis, Elvis. The teds were stamping their feet and chanting, and the police were swinging their truncheons. Johnny Angelo was dancing in the aisle and his flick knife was out and ready:

"Come on," he was screaming, "come on, come right ahead."

A woman had fallen under the seats and was being trampled on.

"Come on," shouted Johnny Angelo, and a big policeman made a run at him; Elvis was still gyrating and blood, blood, Angelo struck, he dug his knife deep in the policeman's belly and screwed it. The man doubled up and fell, his blood jumping up in a spout.

"Johnny," said Catsmeat, "I have to go to the toilet."

"Coppers, coppers," yelled Johnny Angelo, "come and get it."

But Catsmeat had lost him, couldn't find him and was whining for him in the dark. Johnny, where are you? Johnny, I have to go... It can't wait. A copper hit him with his truncheon and Catsmeat collapsed sandbagged underneath the seats. And Johnny Angelo had already forgotten all about the screws. He was looking for the Weasel.

Blood and then more blood; Elvis had stopped singing and was having a love scene but no one, nobody realised. Bodies were lying up and down the aisles, or slung over the seats, or fallen in the rows, and the knives were still gleaming, red on the blades. The screws were out-numbered and humiliated, and the teds were stamping on the beat a battlecry of triumph and total victory. El Vis, El Vis, El Vis.

But someone wasn't stamping, the Weasel he was shouting Down Elvis, Bill Haley is the King. And his gang was with him, fourteen teds and they were booing and chanting Down Elvis, Bill Haley is the King. Johnny Angelo ran towards them.

There was blood on his arm and his leather jeans were soaked in blood. He was tired and sated and still he ran to fight. The Weasel was standing at the top of the aisle, legs apart and his knife ready, and Angelo couldn't get to him; the way was blocked with bodies, and screaming stampeding women were trying to get out.

"Johnny Angelo, where are you?" shouted the Weasel.

"Are you chicken? Can't you take it? Johnny Angelo!" he shouted. "Johnny Angelo!"

It echoed round the cinema: Johnny Angelo, Johnny Angelo.

And Angelo ran at him.

"Gangway!" he yelled, cutting through the struggling bodies. The Weasel's white face was gleaming in the dark and he was balancing on his toes, tense and circling, fencing, backing away. Johnny Angelo ran straight up to him with his knife held out stiff in front of him and he ran right through him, no fencing, no tactics, he ran straight up and through, and dug his knife deep into the Weasel's guts, deep, deep, and he twisted, dug deeper and in one movement pulled out and ran on as the Weasel fell. The Weasel had no time to scream, and Angelo ran straight on out of the cinema and into the street and the shocking silence, blood dripping off his arm. He tripped over his own feet and fell on his knees.

"Elvis is the King," he said.

11 The Flagpole

From the time of his birth Johnny Angelo lived the life of a
hero. An Errol Flynn or a Rudolph Valentino, an Elvis Presley
or a Buffalo Bill Cody. He wanted to be a superman. That was
always the most important thing about him.

When he was sixteen, he climbed a one hundred and twenty
foot flagpole in the full heat of a summer Saturday afternoon.
He shinned up by his hands and feet, no ropes or gadgets, and
the sun shone down brightly on him. At the foot of the flagpole
a crowd of almost one hundred gathered to watch him fall and
kill himself. They stood in a ragged circle, their mouths wide
open, craning their necks upwards. Policemen pushed them
back and shouted for Johnny Angelo to come down. But he
wouldn't. Girls aged thirteen or fourteen clutched each other,
weeping and screaming: Johnny, Johnny. Johnny Angelo kept
climbing, smoothly, calmly, at a steady pace. His hands were
raw and blistered and splinters were sticking into his fingers,
but he kept climbing. At one hundred feet he paused and
seemed to wobble—Ooh, said the crowd, and Johnny, screamed the girls, he's falling, look he's falling, he's going to kill
himself. But he wasn't falling; he was climbing again, and he
went on climbing until he reached the top. And when finally he
did reach the top, he sat and looked out over the city and the
parks and the markets and factories below, and he looked
down into the mouths of the crowd and waved. He pulled out a
wad of paper stickers from his breast pocket and let them
flutter down. The crowd rushed to pick them up, fighting
among themselves, spitting and kicking and scratching.
Angelo smiled benignly down. On each sticker there was a
name, the same name: Johnny Angelo. On white paper in big
black letters: Johnny Angelo. That man again.

He still lived in the tiny room with no heating. But he used
to go back to his family for Sunday lunch. It was a great ritual.
Angelo put on his only grey suit, and his only white shirt, black
tie and square-toed shoes. He brushed his hair flat across his

forehead and he went easy on the hair-oil and he didn't let his forelock fall forward in his eyes. He was sixteen and handsome. Full of dignity.

His mother's front room had been tidied and redecorated. The bed was newly made, the pillowcase had been changed. It was quite nice really, he had to admit that. Quite tidy and fresh.

Angelo stood just inside the door, shifting from foot to foot, and his mother kissed him, once, twice, on the cheeks, very passionately.

"Johnny," she said, "Johnny, how are you? How are you getting on?"

There were little sentimental tears at the corners of her eyes.

"Hello, mother," said Johnny Angelo, lightly.

She was leading him by the hand, tugging him towards the sofa and clutching at him as if he was going to run away.

"Oh Johnny," she said. "What are you doing with yourself? Tell me."

"I'm going to school, mother."

"Are you enjoying yourself?"

"Yes," he said. "I'm enjoying myself."

"Are you taking care of yourself?"

"Yes, I'm taking care of myself."

"Are you eating? Are you keeping your strength up?"

She was wearing her best and most modest black dress and she wasn't biting her nails. She had done her hair specially for him.

"Are you eating enough?" she asked. "Tell me everything, I want to know everything."

She sat on her made-up bed, sitting stiffly forward with her knees pressed tight together and her two hands entwined in her lap. She was so nervous that it was painful to watch her.

"I want you to tell me everything. Everything," she repeated.

The room didn't smell any more. It was tidied and spotless. And his mother was sitting there in front of him, prattling on trying not to weep.

"Oh," said Angelo, "this and that, this and that. I persevere. I do my best."

"But what? Tell me," she said. "Tell me. Tell me what's going to happen next."

"I'm looking around. I don't know yet, it's hard to say."

He saw his sisters in the same room, sitting primly straight-backed like spinsters. There were flies still on the window-panes. But there were no stains on the carpet.

At lunch there was roast leg of lamb and roast potatoes and peas, overcooked and dry, but there, on the table, steaming. And cranberry jelly in a saucer.

"Oh, I remember," his mother said, "how you used to love cranberry jelly when you were little, oh you used to love it so much. You wouldn't eat your dinner without it. Oh, you were a scream at times, you made me laugh so much."

"Yes," said Johnny Angelo, "I remember."

But he didn't; it wasn't like that, it wasn't like that at all, it was horrible and smelly and sordid, that's why he had left.

"Yes," said Johnny Angelo, sweetly sentimental, "I remember. And my father used to like it too, didn't he? Yes he did. I remember you telling me. You told me he loved cran-berry jelly with his Sunday lunch, he wouldn't eat without it."

Lies. All lies.

"Yes," his mother said, "that's right, you're quite right, oh what a memory you have."

And Angelo smiled, his sisters smiled, his mother smiled and dabbed at her eyes and sniffed and smiled again.

"Oh, Johnny," said his mother, "you're all right, aren't you? You are eating enough?"

"Yes, mother," said Johnny Angelo, "I'm doing fine. Just fine."

But then there was another Sunday, a different one, and Johnny Angelo was all dressed up again, and again he hovered just inside the front room door. But the room wasn't tidy this time, the bed wasn't made, the smell was back again. And there was a man in his mother's bed, covered with blankets, a shapeless mound under the sheets. Angelo backed away.

But his mother ran to kiss him, and she pressed him in tight to her.

"Johnny," she exclaimed, "Oh Johnny, how are you? Are you all right? Are you?"

"Am I eating enough?"

"Yes," she said, "are you eating enough?"

The room was full of the smell of sex.

"Who's he?"

"Oh, Johnny. Oh, Johnny, I hope you like him. I do hope

you like him."

In his father's bed. Fat and snoring in his father's bed, stinking the place out. And his mother bleating and clasping her hands like some half-crazed religious maniac.

On the mantelpiece, no portrait of his father. And his mother still clutching at his arm, whining, moaning.

"It's not like that," she was saying, "it's different, it's different."

And Johnny Angelo put on a grim face and said:

"Different? How different? Different like all the others?" he said, "different like the other five thousand?"

"No no no," his mother said, "not like that, it's different. Entirely different."

She was searching feverishly in her mind for the right phrase, for what it really was like.

"It's different," she said. "Like your father."

"Like my father?"

"Yes," she said, "like that." No, wait, she thought, that's wrong, that doesn't sound right, what have I been and gone and said? "No, no," she said, "not like that, I don't mean like that, I mean..."

She was clinging to him, mauling him, thin and old and grey, her body and her face and her eyes all grey.

"No, not like that," she repeated.

"Evil," said Johnny Angelo and left her.

Evil. Evil.

Evil.

His room was terrible but he was stuck with it. He was on his own.

The house was full of cats. On the landings, in the hallway, on the stairs. Sitting on the windowsills. Sleeping on the beds. Sliding down the bainsters. Purring and whining and screeching. Or mousing—everywhere you trod on a dead mouse. Numberless cats, twenty cats, fifty cats. Siamese, Persian, tabby or marmalade. Black. Black, above all. A world of cats. Cats that were blind. Cats that had lost all their fur. Mangy, underfed cats who were always crying or fighting. Mad cats, cats that had been driven crazy. Filthy cats all over the house. Cats that killed each other as they mated. Great black cats of the kind that Johnny Angelo had always loved.

He would wake up in the mornings and the paraffin heater would have run out of fuel, everything frozen solid, the

window was iced over, and he'd have to go down to the corner
pump for a refill. In the mornings there was no Catsmeat to go
for him. It was a drag.

It would be maybe half past seven, seven o'clock, Johnny
Angelo would haul himself out of bed and pick his way down
through the ranks of sleeping or newly dead cats to the front
door. The smell was unbelievable. The stairways were creaking and rotting and the walls were covered all over, floor to
ceiling, in scrawled obscenities. Tramps came in for a shit in
the middle of the night and were still there in the morning,
sleeping in tattered bundles in the passage. Johnny Angelo
lived in no great style.

Out into the street, shivering. No human beings in sight but
cats everywhere. Hundreds of them. Johnny Angelo was king
ruler in a world of cats. There were cats asleep in the gutters
and cats sprawled out on the pavements, cats crawling on their
bellies and cats sneaking down back alleys. Cats who played
with pieces of string. And dead cats who posed on their backs
with their paws in the air. It was a bleak and unfriendly street,
and the wind swept straight down it into Johnny Angelo's
face. It was weird and creepy—no people, just cats. He walked
to the corner pump and the cats all followed him. Every one of
them, a procession of dozens of cats, half starved and flea-
ridden, ranging out in formation behind him as he walked.
Following him and not making a sound. It made him feel like
the Pied Piper of Hamelin.

In the tenement block across the street there was a very old
woman, eighty years old at least, who believed in the Devil.
Last thing at night she would look under her bed to see if there
were any messengers from Hell there, sent to tempt her. She
bolted her windows and doors against Evil, and she slept with
a crucifix under her pillow. It dominated her life, this fear of
Hell. Early one morning she looked out of her window and the
street was full of cats, and through the middle of them strode
Johnny Angelo, dressed in black leather. The old woman
fainted.

The next morning at the same time she looked again and
again the street was full of cats, black cats, and again they
were led by Johnny Angelo. Dressed in black leather, head to
toe; beautiful and arrogant and sinister, a messenger from
Hell; disciple of the Devil himself. He walked the streets when
no one was about, when the city was deserted. Operated in the

secret hours of the night. And drew behind him an army of black cats, lost souls metamorphosed, tormented souls in their death agonies. Souls that were diseased and scarred and dying as the cats themselves were. Johnny Angelo walked slowly to the corner and the cats followed him, every one of them; not one was able to hold back. The old woman saw it all and she knelt down before the Virgin and prayed. Prayed for hours on end. For herself, and for the lost souls of the black cats.

Johnny Angelo was a servant of the Devil. Even at this time, he was already drawing souls towards perdition.

He had an idea.

He bought ten cans of cat meat and poured paraffin into them. Then he went downstairs and scattered the poisoned meat in the street. Very early one morning, about seven o'clock, and there was hoar frost everywhere. Mad with hunger, the cats jumped on the meat and didn't give a damn what it tasted of. They fought over it, they hissed and scratched. They tore each other's eyes out for an extra grain, they killed and killed until there were more cats dead than alive. The black cats were tougher and more determined than the others, and they were killers by instinct. In two minutes the meat was gone, all of it, and only black cats were left standing in the street.

Johnny Angelo went from cat to cat then and held a lighted match to the mouth of each one in turn. It worked.

It really did work. The old woman parted her curtains and the street was full of burning cats. Black cats with red eyes and flaming mouths. That twisted and screamed as the fire ate up their bodies, and turned black cats to red. She closed her curtains fast, the old woman, she shut her eyes. But much too late, of course. She couldn't forget just like that... black cats that turned red. The street lit bright by burning cats.

Or Johnny Angelo presiding. Smiling so benignly on death.

12 The Queen

One thing about Johnny Angelo no one could deny—he hated homosexuals. It was his opinion that homosexuals should be castrated for the first offence and killed outright for any subsequent deviations. Though castration ought to do the trick.

He stood in the lavatory of a pub one time and a man aged about twenty-five and quite good-looking, with dyed blond hair and heavy mascara and thick red lipstick, came up to him. Ham-acting.

"Darling," he said. "Darling, I think you're so gorgeous, I think you look so big and strong. Oh yes," he said, "you do, you do." And he gasped and flap-flap, he fluttered his eye-lashes.

"Oooh," he said, "your muscles. Fun. Would you like some fun?"

Angelo just looked at him, couldn't believe he'd heard what he had heard. He was scared stiff. He ran for it. He stood out in the bar, drinking Scotch neat, and Fun, he thought, Fun, how dare he say Fun to me. And he ran back into the can again. The Queen was standing in front of the mirror, applying more lipstick, and Johnny Angelo ran up behind him and jabbed him hard in the back.

"Ooh," said the queen, jumped and turned round; his flies were undone, he had deliberately left his cock hanging out. Angelo backed away; the queen tittered and screamed. Johnny Angelo got mad, he had his flick knife out again, yet again, tight-faced and screaming blue murder, and he was closing in.

"Oh," said the queen, "oh, ooh, oooohhh..." and backed away, slid away, he was shielding himself with his hands, he backed away, moaning softly, ooh, ooohh, until his back was hard against the wall. The wall was bright shining white tiles, the strip lighting was bright, white. Johnny Angelo followed him with his knife held out, slipped in after him.

"Ponce," he said, "dirty lousy fag."

He cut sideways and downwards, slashed, sss; the queen jumped back and the knife went past him. No one moved. The lights were so bright and the shining tiles on the wall, it was like being in an operating theatre.

The queen gave a little moan, a tiny scream and tried to back away again. Angelo was in after him, brought his knife down and caught the side of the queen's hand, just a flesh would, nothing serious, but it brought a lot of blood. The queen stopped running; he just stood there and looked. Looked at Johnny Angelo, stared at him, and he was too scared and hurt to scream but his face was white and his eyes were huge, the pupils filled the whole eye. He looked like a rabbit. Stared, stared, and Angelo was going to cut again but couldn't, those big staring eyes paralysed him and he couldn't do a thing. He ran. Ran again, ran out of the can, out of the pub, running blindly along the street.

"Queen," he said, "dirty queen, dirty screaming queen," he leaned up against a wall, puked up all of his guts onto the pavement. Knelt down and spewed. And went on retching when he had nothing left to vomit.

Sick of fags and sick of everything. Sick of living in his filthy room, sick of all dirt and squalor. Sick of being in contact with the kind of sordid people that lived all around him. Sick of people, period.

He had to get out. He decided to be a singer. And he bought himself a guitar.

There was a club down in the dockland, the Blue Suede Shoes. It was down in a basement, and it was dark and dirty like any other cellar club. Poky. The kids came roaring in around midnight on their black mobikes, teds who had long greasy hair and dirty finger-nails and faces like weasels. And their girls who were always blonde and whose breasts were big and bulging under tight sweaters that didn't fit. They packed out the Suede Shoes every night, smoking but not drinking, just sipping at Coca-Cola and frothy capuccino. They were orderly, genteel. They kept their cool. The big thing was chain-smoking; each of them had his own cool and style in dragging or flicking ash, each one was an artist, and the girls sat round and watched and they were all after the same one boy, the boy who was the coolest with a cigarette, so was the ritual; the boys chain-smoked to save their lives, the girls sat round and did nothing. There were cutting contests that lasted all night and the one who won, the really cool one, was King until someone could come along to beat him. They lived by filter tips the way you can live by stud poker or pool. The cigarette King was absolute.

They sat on barrels and on crates, in the cold and dark, and there was a tiny stage at one end of the cellar, ten foot by six. Johnny Angelo was booked in to play at thirty shillings a night.

The first night, he came in early. The teds were smoking, it was a major contest, the King against his challenger. Johnny Angelo stood by the door and watched. The teds sat round in a tight circle and didn't talk, didn't move, hardly dare to breathe. All you could see were two thin columns of smoke, rising slowly and diluting. And two pairs of hands stirring on opposite sides of a beer barrel, hands rising slowly to the mouth, curving and holding still. Or wrists that didn't move a millimetre for five minutes, and then flashed once in the dark, very suddenly, striking like a rattlesnake, and were still again. No sound. No movement. Just the four hands moving and the two rising columns of smoke.

Then, quite without warning, one of the smokers threw down his fag-end and ground his heel on it. Walked away from the circle and hid. The King sat back and took one long, deep drag. Still King. The girls moved in closer to him.

Johnny Angelo came forward into the light. His heels banged down on the floor and the teds turned to meet him, and he stood above them and looked down. Looked down on them in arrogance and amusement. The King stood up to meet him and his face came under the light. It was the Weasel.

"The Weasel," said Johnny Angelo. "You remember me?"

"Johnny Angelo."

"Elvis is still the King," said Johnny Angelo.

They faced each other, squaring up. The two of them were standing and everyone else was sitting.

"Sport," said Johnny Angelo, "do you smoke?"

"I smoke," said the Weasel.

"For how much?"

"For my one hundred fags against yours."

They sat down on opposite sides of the beer barrel, and on the top of the barrel were littered two hundred cigarettes. They looked at each other, Johnny Angelo and the Weasel, and tried to stare each other down. The Weasel's supporters

ranged in ranks behind him. And Catsmeat stood alone behind
Johnny Angelo.

They smoked.

There were four standards for judging. One: the style in
which the cigarette was brought to the mouth and the drag
itself was performed. Two: the depth to which the smoke was
inhaled and the length of time it remained in the lung without
the contestant choking. Three: the smoothness with which the
smoke was then exhaled, the quantity of smoke itself and the
condition of the contestant immediately after, e.g. no gasping,
watery eyes, etc. Four: the style of wrist-flick with which the
ash was finally broken off the butt. It was a detailed science.

How to describe it? When so little happened. Johnny
Angelo was a stylist; his initial action and his final wrist-flick
were the next thing to miraculous. The Weasel was more in
practice; he held smoke with great ease and his lungs were like
indiarubber. They smoked in silence and neither would give
way.

They finished the first cigarette and went on to the second.
They finished the second cigarette and went on to the third.
Neither was wilting. Neither was better than the other. The
crowd was standing closer, breathing less, and neither Johnny
Angelo nor the Weasel was willing to lose. The third cigarette.
Tension. Concentration. They crouched in the dark and
smoked.

It ended very suddenly, very quietly. The Weasel tried to
hold his smoke too long and choked. The rope snapped, the
tension dissolved. The Weasel got up from the table and
walked away, no longer King. And no one followed him.

There was nothing for the Weasel to do. He walked out of
the club, went up the stairs and surfaced into the dockland,
and he didn't come back. Johnny Angelo again, he thought.
Everything he touched was shattered by Johnny Angelo.

And Angelo controlled the field. He had it made.

No one moved at all. Johnny Angelo sat very still, his hands
in his pockets, his feet on the barrel, letting his cigarette run
down between his fingers. Catsmeat counted out the winn-
ings. And that was all. It was an anticlimax.

And very slowly, unwillingly almost, the teds began to drift
round the barrel until they were standing behind Johnny
Angelo. Everything was changed. They had a new leader. It
took some getting used to; it took time to take it in. And they

waited patiently for Johnny Angelo to come out of his day-
dream, to make a move. They wanted to be told what to do.

The girls moved in closer to him. Closer, closer, until they
were almost touching him. And the Weasel wasn't the King
now, Bill Haley wasn't the King. Even Elvis Presley wasn't
the King. Johnny Angelo was the King.

Johnny Angelo.

13 The Blue Suede Shoes

Johnny Angelo was the King.

It was a very great change in his life, it was maybe the most important thing that ever happened to him. Johnny Angelo, leader of men.

He was seventeen years of age and in all that time he had always been a lone wolf, a solitary. Completely isolated from everyone. Now suddenly he had followers who hung around just to obey his orders. And girls who lived only to make love to him. All because he could smoke a cigarette without choking. It took a lot of getting used to.

He was big time suddenly. He was top dog, he had it made. He was the King.

And he was a rock 'n roll singer at this club, the Blue Suede Shoes.

He wore a gold lamé suit with blue velvet trimmings and lapels. And matching gold shoes with blue velvet laces. And he carried a gold-plated guitar shaped like a spaceship, slung around his waist, and he swung it like a giant phallus from side to side as he sang. He didn't know how to play it properly but he strummed on it and banged on the boards and sang and shouted over the top of it. And no one was analysing his guitar technique.

They were watching his legs instead. He had great long skinny beanpole legs which sprawled across the stage and became like rubber the minute he began to move. They bent double, they stretched like elastic, they twisted back underneath him or they swivelled round to face the wrong way. Puppet legs, spider legs. The fastest legs in the world, that spelled out sex.

There were no screams and no demonstrations. His followers sat in the dark and stared at his legs. They sat on orange crates and beer barrels and all he could see of them were the tips of their cigarettes glowing in the dark. They didn't make a sound. They didn't clap or stamp, they didn't even applaud at the end of numbers; they listened in total silence. No whispering, no clinking of glasses, no matches striking. It could have been a church.

Johnny Angelo sang on a tiny raised stage at the far end of the room and his legs filled every inch of it.

It was an act of worship. Johnny Angelo was the high priest, the witch doctor. Or, rather, not Johnny Angelo, just his legs. Ridiculous and frightening and entertaining and hypnotic, all at the same moment. Skinny legs that were far too long, tight in gold lamé. And no one listened to the music, no one watched Johnny Angelo, they just stared straight ahead at these two long swivelling, gyrating legs. His legs took on the whole of Johnny Angelo's personality, arrogant, sexual, exhibitionist. They slithered from side to side, twisted themselves into knots, leapt high in the air, turned to jelly. Ran, cowered, kicked, flaunted. A single light shone on him, the only light in the place, and followed him wherever he moved, until his legs were the only thing you could see, and they began to grow bigger and away from the body, and finally became the legs of a god, a giant. You hadn't the strength left to look away, or close your eyes; you just had to stare at Johnny Angelo's legs. The signifying legs of Johnny Angelo.

Every night, the same routine. Johnny Angelo sang in the Blue Suede Shoes, and his followers sat with the lights out and watched his legs. It was obsessive.

He hypnotised them. He turned them into morons, robots, capable of doing only what he told them to do and thinking only what he told them to think. Ants, drone bees; they existed to follow him, and to obey his orders, to worship him. They were tough guys, great hulking red-faced teds in black leather; but Johnny Angelo came along and they crumbled into so many Catsmeats. He could be frightening, that kid. King Johnny Angelo.

They went roadriding at night on their mobikes. Johnny Angelo led the cavalcade, leader of the pack.

He would come out of the Suede Shoes at maybe two o'clock in the morning, in the depths of the night, and take them riding on the clearways and ring roads.

It was dead quiet in the dockland, quiet as a graveyard. There was no one about and the ships were tied up at dock, the crews all asleep. A beautiful clear night, total silence. Nothing stirred. And then suddenly out of nothing, there was a great roar, a roar of one engine, two, three, then ten and twenty, kicking into life, revving up. The whole docklands were shattered in one moment, windows shook in their frames, loose bricks broke free and fell crashing into the street. The ground itself shook, great tremors passed through the stone. It could have been an earthquake. It could have been judgement day, the end of the world.

Out of the roar of the engines emerged Johnny Angelo. In black leather and a black crash helmet and on his back there was a silver dragon emblazoned and the single word ELVIS. He rode up to the front and the parade began to roll. Very slowly, soberly, up out of the docklands and into the city streets, right through the city centre. A solemn procession, stately. Johnny Angelo led the pack. Catsmeat rode close behind him, just over his right shoulder. And behind them, twenty or thirty more, fanned out in formation, riding slowly through the middle of town.

Nightriders: a long stately procession rolling through the empty night-town. All in black leather, all with black crash helmets. And on the back of each one of them an emblazoned silver dragon. And the single word ELVIS. Messengers from Hell. Disciples of the Devil. The followers of Johnny Angelo.

It was a ghost town. Streets which were always crowded, shops which were full and pavements which overflowed, tonight were completely deserted. Streets which always looked too small and cramped to hold their traffic, tonight were huge and empty. It was like a town that had been stricken with plague, or a town you walk through in a dream. And the only sound in the whole city was the sound of purring engines. Nothing to look at, nothing to see. But the line of thirty riders, black for evil, who rode through town, not looking to the left or the right, riding straight ahead.

On to the clearways and they started to go. The growl of the engines went up into a shrill whine, thirty pairs of high black boots, thirty pairs of goggles, sixty frog eyes. Ton-up: outside town there was a long straight stretch, a slow hill that rose gently for nearly two miles and then they swept up over the brow and down the other side and went, went, as if their lives depended on it. It was a wonderful thing to see, if you were approaching from the opposite direction. Coming to the end of the straight, nearly at the break in the hill, you could already hear the engines, the thunder, the roar. Then the first one

breasted the hill, Johnny Angelo, he reached the crest and
soared off straight into space, the death leap, he hit the top of
the hill and he flew, twenty, thirty, maybe forty feet before he
hit the ground again; and you were right underneath him, he
leaped straight up above you, King Johnny Angelo, in black
leather on a black machine, and rising above you he was huge,
he was superhuman, a giant, a vision; you didn't have time to
take him in before the next one followed him, Catsmeat, and
the next, and the next, racing up to the crest and jumping
straight into nothing, twenty of them, thirty, and not one of
them faltered, not for a second. You turned around and
watched them go, and Johnny Angelo was already half a mile
down the road, way up over the ton and pushing, pushing, all
the time; you'd think he wanted to kill himself. That's the kind
of thing you don't ever forget.

Nightrider. Johnny Angelo roamed the countryside like a
phantom, perched on his mobike like a great black bird. As
dawn came closer, he wheeled around and returned to the city.
He rode through the empty streets while everyone was sleeping and sank down into the dockland. Down, down to the very
edge of the water, to the Blue Suede Shoes; where the door
opened for him and he disappeared without trace into the
earth from which he had come.

He had his own room in the back of the club, a room carved
out of the centre of the earth. No windows, no air, but there
were dark lights and plushy cushions and seductive music to
be switched on by pressing a button. It was soft and scented
and sexual, the room of a seducer, as snug as a womb.

Johnny Angelo's headquarters. No arthritic, rheumatic
room in a tenement slum for Johnny Angelo now; no fetching
of paraffin from the corner pump at seven in the morning,
while the neighbourhood cats bickered at his heels. He was
well looked after here. He was coddled, he was the King. And
in the Blue Suede Shoes the word meant something. Johnny
Angelo was treated at all times as a king deserved.

He read up Breakfasts in the glossy magazines, and insisted
on the very best. His bed was covered in burnt-orange cusions
and, when his minions brought him his breakfast in the mornings, he had grapefruit and ginger, croissants, cheese-cake.
He wasn't taking second best again.

He was brought his morning paper on a silver salver. And
next to the paper there was his morning cigarette; it was put in

the holder, the long holder was placed in his mouth, the match
was struck for him, the cigarette was lit. All he had to do for
himself was breathe.

Doors were opened in front of him and closed again behind
him. His followers would rise to him whenever he came into a
room and not sit down again until he told them to. The girls
would open their legs for him any time he wanted, any time,
they were glad to. The boys would spend their days polishing
up his black mobike, improving the acceleration, tightening
the brakes, polishing, polishing. Their lives revolved around
him, their days and weeks were taken up with him. He was the
Sun. The little red rooster.

He was improving his education now, learning long words
which Catsmeat didn't understand.

"It is the mentality of a star," said Johnny Angelo. "It is
fated that they are pursued with worship and idolisation."

"Certainly," said Catsmeat. "Certainly it is."

Johnny Angelo got up on stage one night and began to
shake his legs, and immediately he sensed that there was
someone new out there in the dark, a stranger, someone who
didn't belong, someone who wasn't thinking right about him.
A girl. He told Catsmeat to bring her to him in his room.

Catsmeat went over to her and sat down.

"Johnny Angelo wants you," he said. "He wants to see
you."

"Who?" said the girl. "Who's that?"

Catsmeat couldn't see her. Her voice came to him out of the
dark, and it was low and cool and sexy, it made his hair bristle
up and down the back of his neck.

"Johnny Angelo," he said. "The singer."

And she came, she came to Johnny Angelo's room with
Catsmeat and the light shone on her face. She was a coloured
chick.

She was dark, really dark, a deep tan brown, and she was
long and lean, supple, and her skin was smooth. Johnny
Angelo thought she was just beautiful.

"Good evening," he said. "My name is Johnny Angelo and
I am pleased to make your acquaintance."

"Good evening," she said. Pretty. Polite. Nice teeth, good
bones.

"May I offer you a drink?"

"Thank you."

"And may I offer you something to eat?"

"Yes," she said. "Olives and anchovies. Smoked salmon rolls."

And she ate them as if she lived on them, as if she never touched anything else. She was very cool, very self-possessed for a shine, and her voice made Johnny Angelo crack his knuckles. He was deeply impressed.

"May I enquire what your name is?" asked Johnny Angelo.

"Yolande," she said. "My name is Yolande."

"A very pretty name."

"Thank you."

"For a very pretty girl."

"Thank you," she said, but not as if she meant it. She behaved as if she met a Johnny Angelo every day of the week and swallowed them with her elevenses. As if he was small change from sixpence.

He blushed.

"For a very pretty girl indeed," he said.

"Yes."

"For the prettiest girl I've met in a long time." He was sitting in his cushions and smoking cigarettes through a long holder. The hi-fi was purring, the lights were way down low. Breasts, thought Johnny Angelo, just look at her.

She was sitting with her hands crossed in her lap, waiting for the next move. It was true, she was beautiful, she was truly lovely.

"Yolande," said Johnny Angelo. "Yolande." Rolling it on his tongue, savouring it. Yolande. Yolande.

She waited. She made no move of her own.

"Is the drink all right for you?"

"Fine."

Johnny Angelo was mule-headed, he wouldn't let go.

"What do you do for a living?" he asked.

"This and that," she said. "I do various things."

"Nice things?"

"Not nice. Not un-nice."

He sat back and took a long pull on his whisky. He tried to stare her down, but she took no notice. She was waiting for him to speak. And he didn't, he wouldn't. Slow down, thought Johnny Angelo; cool it; play it her way. Keep your mouth shut, he thought; beat her at her own game.

So he put it on ice.

He didn't speak. He lay back in his cushions and looked her over. Took a good long look at her breasts. Calculated her thighs. Arrogant and contemptuous, looking her down like so much horseflesh. And waiting for her to crack. She was sitting in a high-backed chair by the door. Her back was straight and her knees were tight together, her hands folded on her lap. She looked virginal. She also looked tough.

He waited. She waited. And nothing happened. There was a silence, a deep dead silence, except for the hi-fi purring on in the shadow.

"Have you been here before?" said Johnny Angelo at last.

"Here?"

"The Blue Suede Shoes."

"No," she said. "Never."

"And do you like it? Now that you've seen it?"

"Quite," she said. "I quite like it. I don't dislike it. I wouldn't say it was horrible."

She was as tough as he was, as mule-headed, and as bloody-minded as Johnny Angelo himself. Johnny Angelo was beat, and he knew it. He closed his eyes in depseration.

"Yolande," he said. "Yolande."

"Mmm?"

"Do you like me?"

"I don't know yet."

"Do you think I look good?"

"Yes," she said. "I think you look good."

"Then come here," he said.

"No."

"Come here," repeated Johnny Angelo, a little louder. "Come over here."

"No," said Yolande. "I won't."

"Kiss me."

"No."

"Yes," he said. "Yes, you must."

"No," she said. Very calm, very firm. "No, I won't."

"Bitch!" he shouted. "Bloody whore! Come here, I COMMAND YOU!" But it was too late. She was up and gone, long, gone straight out of the door and away, and she even had the nerve to wave him goodbye as she went. Johnny Angelo was left raging in an empty room, raping the walls.

He was sore, Johnny Angelo; it cut him up pretty bad. It hurt his pride and he wasn't used to that. It left him beaten, too, and he wasn't used to that either.

He sent for Catsmeat.

"Who was that?" he said. "That shine chick. What do you know about her?"

"Yolande? Some whore."

"Whore? What the hell d'you mean, whore? That stupid virgin a whore? Are you out of your tiny cretin mind?"

Catsmeat didn't like the look of this. Johnny Angelo was mad, plenty mad, and red in the face. Catsmeat played it careful.

"Well," he said, "I heard that somewhere, I might be wrong, I wouldn't swear, it might be someone else."

"Who says so?" demanded Johnny Angelo. "Who says so?"

"I don't know," said Catsmeat. "Guys around."

Johnny Angelo turned his back, turned his face away.

"What kind of a whore?" he said. "A real pro?"

"That's what I heard," said Catsmeat. "Someone said that."

He was cowering, bent almost double, his mouth big and wet, his eyes full of tears.

"I heard that," he said. "I might be wrong."

"Shit. You're not wrong," said Johnny Angelo. "Don't give me shit. You know you're not wrong."

"Well..."

"That's right, that's right," said Johnny Angelo. "She's just another whore."

He sat down on his bed and thought about it. Listening to the hi-fi. He was calming down.

"Fancy that," he said. "A whore. Can you beat that? A common bloody whore." He laughed, and chuckled to himself, cupping his chin in his hand.

"Cool operator," he said. "She certainly had me fooled."

Catsmeat came up behind him and snickered in his ear, laughing behind his hand like a six-year-old.

"Mean fuck," he said. "I bet she'd be a real juicy fuck."

Angelo turned his head.

"What?"

Speaking very slowly, he said:

"What? What was that you said?"

Catsmeat walked backwards, retreated, his hands were up in front of his face.

"Johnny," he said. "I didn't, I..."

And bang, Angelo's big hand came down on the side of his head, hard, very hard. Catsmeat dropped on his hands and knees, and his mouth began to bleed. He tried to crawl away.

"I didn't, Johnny," he said. "I wouldn't."

Angelo came after him, slowly, methodically; then his knee came up hard under Catsmeat's chin and turned him head over heels. He crashed into the wall, Catsmeat, head first; he wasn't screaming, he was blubbering, gibbering, whining Johnny, Johnny, Johnny. Angelo kicked him in the ribs, crunch, once, twice, three times. Catsmeat folded up on the floor, trying to pull in his head like a snail. Then he put his arms round Angelo's legs and held them tight, held them there and wept through closed lips, Johnny, Johnny, Johnny.

Angelo pushed him away and didn't hit him any more. He sat down on his bed again and thought for a long time without speaking. Catsmeat crawled away into a corner, rolled up tight into a ball, went on crying. The hi-fi didn't stop playing. Bitch, Johnny Angelo was thinking, the filthy whore, the low-down stinking bitch. He punched his fist into his palm and swore.

No one got away from Johnny Angelo. No one ever. He wouldn't allow it, he refused to permit it. No smart-arsed shine chicks with big ideas got away from Johnny Angelo. He wouldn't have it. He absolutely would not allow it.

He was cracking his knuckles over and over again. He sat with his head down and worked it out.

Johnny Angelo had to be loved. Every woman in the world had to love him. No exception, no arguments. He insisted. And if Yolande wouldn't love him and fuck him, he would see to it that she loved him and gave him something even better. No one escaped him, no one got away. Not even her. Not if he played her right, not if he appealed to her weakness. And her weakness was? Common sense. She had more common sense than anyone Angelo had ever met. If he appealed to her sense of romance, she would laugh in his face, he could see that. But if he fed her a proposition which appealed to her common sense, she would have to accept it. She would have no alternative.

Catsmeat still lay in his corner and wept, muttering Angelo's name, Johnny, Johnny, over and over again. Johnny Angelo was standing over him, looking down. And he was smiling.

"Catsmeat," he said. "I think you're right about her. A mean fuck. A real juicy fuck."

Catsmeat stared at him, blood and spittle oozing out of the corner of his mouth.

"Bring her to me," said Johnny Angelo. "I want to see her."

She was something completely new in his life, Yolande, the first woman he had met with the power to think for herself. And he liked her for it. Hated her for it, certainly, but he also liked her for it. A fuck wasn't worth anything, after all; you fucked someone and that was all, you discarded her again. But someone like this, a thinker, a hard dealer, she deserved something better. Something closer and more lasting. Something that Johnny Angelo really cared about.

Catsmeat went to find her and she came without hesitation, unworried by the first time. She sat on the same high-backed chair, her hands folded in the same way. Nothing had changed; the hi-fi was playing. Johnny Angelo was lying back in his cushions and eating black grapes. She waited.

"Yolande," he said. "I wish to make you an apology."

Johnny Angelo, who had never made an apology to anyone from the day he was born. Yolande inclined her head towards him in gracious forgiveness.

"I misjudged you," said Johnny Angelo. "I freely admit that. I took you to be like all the others and I was wrong. Because you are not like all the others. You are sharp and you have a mind of your own; I like that. You know just what you want; I also like that. I like a whole lot of things about you."

He was generous and a little patronising; he was doing her favours.

"Yes," he said. "I believe I could do many things that would help you."

"No," said Yolande. "I don't want anything. Thank you very much. I don't need anyone."

Johnny Angelo raised his hand for silence, slightly offended.

"I wouldn't suggest that for a moment," he said. "I wouldn't be so crude."

He paused, and wet his ?ips.

"I am going to be a star," he said. "That is a known fact. I am going to be famous and I am going to be rich, I am going to be a very big star. I will need a secretary. I will need some kind of housekeeper. I will need someone to keep my affairs in order, to take the routine things off my mind. I will need someone to manage my home, to check my appointments, to control my financial affairs. Things like that, all this type of business. And you can do it, Yolande," said Johnny Angelo graciously. "I believe you have the capacity to do it."

"Do what?" she said. "Be your nursemaid? Change your nappy for you?"

"At, let us say, a basic salary of twenty pounds a week?"

She sat very still, giving no sign of liking it or not liking it. Angelo waited.

"Well," she said. "I..."

Got her, he thought. Got her cold, he thought, got her right where I want her. Caught her. Trapped her. Wrapped up tight in the web.

"Well," he said. "What do you say?"

She pretended to be thinking about it.

"The way I see it," she said, "you don't want me to be your secretary. You want me to be your mum."

And Johnny Angelo smiled and stretched, knowing he had her, knowing she wouldn't get away.

"Well," he said, "and why not? Why the hell not?"

"Yes," she said, defeated. "Why not?"

14 The Tyrant

Johnny Angelo was an operator. Yolande thought she was
smart but she wasn't as sharp as she looked. She thought she
had Angelo all wrapped up, but indeed he had her wound right
round his finger all the time.

She was born to act mother to Johnny Angelo. On the first
day she turned up hard and cynical about the whole thing; at
the end of a week she was hooked. She lived to look after him.
She brought him his breakfast in bed, laid out his new day's
clothes at the foot of the bed, made his bed after him. Then
she washed up the breakfast things, swept out his room,
hoovered the floor, dusted, and made him his mid-morning
cup of tea. So on and so on without rest, right through the day.

And why did she put up with it? Because she wanted to and
needed to. Because she was impervious to sex but defenceless
against slavery. Because she was born to serve Johnny
Angelo.

At nights she lay alone in her bed but couldn't sleep for the
noise Johnny Angelo made in the next room. And in the morning he had left his used condom on the floor for her to clear
away; she had to pick it up in her fingers and carry it dripping
to the waste basket. To look at Angelo's cold sperm when all
passion was gone from it was the closest she got to his love.

She hated him. He filled her life, the hate of him, the loath-
ing, the plans for revenge. He made her strip-tease when he
had company. He made her sleep with his friends. But he
didn't deign to lay her himself.

Because he was shrewd. Because he knew that if he laid her,
she would get free, she would be just another screw and no
more use to him. So she had to do without. She was of more
use to him as she was. She came into his room in the morning
and lifted up her nightdress for him. She was very beautiful.
But Johnny Angelo laughed in her face and told her to go
away. He did no one favours.

At the end of three weeks he didn't pay her salary. Yolande

came storming into his room and spat into his eyes.

"Shit!" she said. "Shit, you evil lump of shit, you didn't pay me! You said you'd pay me and you didn't."

Johnny Angelo laughed.

"Am I to take it that you are dissatisfied?"

"Dissatisfied fuck," said Yolande. "Pay me, you bastard, just pay me."

"If you are dissatisfied," said Johnny Angelo, "I would suggest that you leave."

What could she do? She stayed.

She hated him. She hated him till her face went ash grey and she had to dig her nails into her flesh to stop herself screaming. She hated him twenty-four hours a day, plotted against him, and in her dreams she saw herself killing Johnny Angelo. She hated him. He called her into his room and told her he'd found dust on the mantelpiece, or that the bed was made wrong. Niggled, criticised, made her do everything again. He told her she was an ugly, idle cow.

She bought a jar of aspirins and crumbled them into his tea. She took it in to him and he drank it.

"Jesus," he said, "this is horrible, this is disgusting. Why the hell does it taste so bitter?"

Yolande stood over him and smiled, smooth and beautiful.

"Because I put poison in it," she said.

"Poison?"

"Yes," she said. "I thought I'd had just about enough of you. I thought it was time to make a change."

Johnny Angelo went very pale. A ring of sweat broke out on his forehead. He put his hand down to his belly, his guts clenched. The first fierce spasm of pain ran through him and his face creased in agony. His mouth went big and wet, hanging open, and his eyes popped, he got to his feet and staggered, limped halfway across the floor, collapsed in a heap and writhed and twisted on the floor, kicking his feet in the air, thrashing around him. But not whining, not screaming; that would have been unmanly. Yolande stood over him.

"Like it?" she said. "How do you like it?"

He didn't. He lay very still on the floor and his face was ivory white and cold sweat was running off him in waves. His eyes were wide open, staring up at her. His clenched fists began slowly to relax. He thought he was dying.

"How do you like it?" said Yolande. "Is it fun?"

His lips were cold and blue. They moved slowly and painfully.

"Bitch," he said. "Murderess. Filthy murdering bitch, I
damn you to Hell and hope you burn."

He was talking calmly, tonelessly, very faintly.

"Bitch, I put a curse on you. I hope you burn in Hell."

Yolande was kneeling at his side, cradling his head in her
arms, stroking him, pressing him to her bosom. Big salt tears
were running down her cheeks, and dripping off the end of her
nose.

"Johnny," she said. "Forgive me, Johnny, oh forgive me.
Please, Johnny, please."

Like the last reel of an old-style Western... and Johnny
Angelo sat up and smiled, then got on his feet and walked
away. He drank off the rest of his tea and made a face.

"Do yourself a favour," he said, "don't play games."

She lost again.

He gave her a pound to get in some shopping, and she gave
him eight shillings change. He sat down and worked out the
bill penny by penny.

"Cheat," he said, "lousy cheat, you cheated me."

She was three pennies short. He stood in the middle of the
room and screamed, cheat, cheat, cheat.

He believed he was being watched. He thought that his life
was in danger.

He hid behind his curtains and watched the street outside.
The street was completely deserted, and the wind blew fallen
leaves along the pavements. In the shadow of a house on the
far side, a man was waiting and smoking a cigarette.

"Look," said Johnny Angelo, "look at that. Just take a look
at that."

"What?" said Yolande. "What are you talking about?"

"Spies."

He sent two of his strong-arm men to follow the man. He led
them to a bedsitter in one of the city slums. And at four in the
morning he was found in a phone box by a policeman on the
beat, badly beaten up. His face had been slashed with razors.

Spies: Johnny Angelo was being watched. He was being
followed. There were plots against his life.

He was getting edgy. His nerves were as sensitive as newly
drilled teeth. He would lie awake in the night and not be able
to sleep. Toss and turn. Eat his heart out. Then he would get

up and pad over to the window and look out. Nothing, the
street was empty. And then he would see it: a cigarette glowing in the dark, a shifting shadow. And he would know he was
being watched. He could do nothing without being watched.

In the Blue Suede Shoes one night, in his dressing-room, he
went to the wardrobe to take out his gold lamé suit and it had
been razor-slashed. At the knee and waist and shoulder,
ripped to shreds. And a bottle of indelible ink had been flung
over the remnants. Kaput, his beautiful golden suit. It was the
end of so much. Johnny Angelo held the ruined suit in his
arms and rocked it like a baby and solemnly swore revenge.

And how much later was it? Three or four nights, a week
perhaps—his mobike was tampered with. The engine choked
up and began to fail on the big fast straight at the top of the
hill, and Angelo, instead of heading the cavalcade as he
always did, had to brake and tail off and trail in last. It was
humiliating.

They weren't very important things maybe, not dangerous
or significant, but they were destructive and undignified and
they made out Johnny Angelo to be less than he was, they
lessened his authority as leader. For these reasons he felt himself unable to let them pass. He was forced to take action. He
made out an alphabetical list of the members of his gang, A to
Z, and one by one he called them into his room and sat them in
the seat where Yolande had sat, the hot seat. The boy would
be sweating and nervous. Johnny Angelo lay back in his
cushions and ate figs, staring the boy up and down, making
him suffer. Then he told him solemnly that there was a traitor
among them, a schemer against the safety of Johnny Angelo.
That his gold suit had been destroyed and his mobike tampered with, and further outrages were inevitably to follow, and
that only one of the gang could possibly be responsible, only
he would have the time and opportunity to do these things.
And so he, Johnny Angelo, had decided he needed protection
and from all the gang he had selected this one boy, this one
among all the others, as the one most worthy of trust, worthy
to be Johnny Angelo's spy and protector. He was relying on
this boy to find out the traitor's identity and report him, so that
together they could stamp him out. Did the boy understand
this?

Yes.

And was he willing to do it?

Yes.

Then Johnny Angelo was personally grateful to him, thanked and commended him, and wished him the very best fortune in his task, god speed.

And the boy would go away glowing with pride and purpose, and Johnny Angelo would call in the next on his list, and the next, and the next, and bullshit each and every one of them in exactly the same manner. Until each of them thought he was watching all the others, believing himself to be the sole defender of Johnny Angelo, so that no one could leave the room or go to the can or scratch his arse without being observed and suspected by upwards of twenty amateur detectives. And the traitor himself believed that he was safe and secure in Johnny Angelo's trust, his right-hand man, beyond suspicion; when, in fact, his every move was being noted and reported back, the net was closing in, he was going to slip up, he was about to get himself caught. He was going to be found out and ground into nothing.

Johnny Angelo congratulated himself; he thought he was a smart operator. He was safe from his gang, therefore safe from the most obvious source of treason. By playing them off against each other in this way he was taking their minds off him. They cancelled each other out; it was a smooth arrangement.

Did it work? Johnny Angelo began to sleep more soundly, he ate well, he started to put on lost weight. He no longer hid behind the curtains and watched the streets. He was more relaxed, more secure inside himself. As smug as a cat with a saucer of milk.

Yolande came to see him, broke down before him and wept. She was never alone for a second. When she went to get the shopping, she was followed inch by inch. When she tried to call a client, she had her phone tapped. And when she went to her room to take her clothes off, she was watched through the keyhole. She wasn't very strong now; her nerves were shot, she was a wreck, she couldn't take it. So she came to Angelo and cried and Yes, she said, she admitted it, she had been to his dressing-room and she had destroyed his beautiful gold suit. It had been her all the time.

Why? he asked her.

Because she had been mad at him. Because he had pushed her too far once and she absolutely had to get her own back on him somehow. It was as simple as that.

It answered one question, it raised another. If the case of the lamé suit was as straightforward as that, did it mean there was a commonplace explanation for everything? Did it mean there was no danger to Johnny Angelo's life after all?

"No," said Johnny Angelo, "I don't believe it."

He believed there was a conspiracy against him, a plot. He believed he was being watched. He believed he was being set up for the kill. He refused to believe otherwise.

Yolande? He took a plain white piece of cardboard and he painted the word VANDAL on it in great black letters so that everyone could see, and he made her walk around with it hung across her back. She was compelled to wear it at all times. So that there was no mistake. So that everyone understood what happened to the enemies of Johnny Angelo.

He walked to the park and stood at the traffic lights, waiting for the lights to change. A car came racing through, a red sports model, and it careered wildly up onto the pavement, heading straight for him. Angelo jumped back. The wheels missed him by maybe six inches, maybe eight, and the car ploughed straight on. Ran back off the pavement and teetered to a stop. Johnny Angelo was crouching against a shop window, covering his head with his arms, and the car had sprayed his trouser-bottoms with white dust. The driver looked back, saw that Johnny Angelo was still alive, and drove on.

"It was an accident," Yolande said. "It was some drunk. It was some hit-and-run bum who didn't have the guts to come back. That's all. I'm sure it wasn't deliberate."

"Accident? Accident nothing," he said. "You know it wasn't. You know damn well it wasn't. It was attempted assassination."

At the age of eighteen the killing of Johnny Angelo was already beyond murder. It had reached the scale of full-blown assassination.

He had proof. They were trying to kill him.

They were trying to kill him because he was successful. Because he was handsome. Because he ran the best gang in town, a gang well worth taking over.

And because he was Johnny Angelo.

Who could be responsible? Who hated him that much? Who was ambitious enough? Who else but the Weasel? The

Weasel, who from the very first had tried to bring Johnny Angelo down, who had schemed before and had been foiled, who had lost everything due to Johnny Angelo. Who else could it be but the Weasel?

For the third time Johnny Angelo against the Weasel.

Johnny Angelo was making time with a girl named Louise.

She sat in the front row to watch him sing, and she showed from her knees right up her thighs to her stocking-tops. But Louise had a jealous man named Sid, who didn't like the way Johnny Angelo was looking at her. Sid went up to Angelo and told him to leave Louise alone. Angelo laughed.

"You know what I think?" said Johnny Angelo. "I think they should call you Greasy Sid. And you know why? Because you're real greasy, that's why."

Greasy Sid. Greasy Sid. He was blown out of Johnny Angelo's presence like a bad smell.

One night Johnny Angelo picked up this girl Louise and took her home to lay her. But he never did get her into bed because, halfway up the alley behind the Blue Suede Shoes, someone jumped out behind him, pulled a knife and stabbed him. The knife went through Angelo's jacket and only nicked his ribs, and Angelo grabbed hold of the knife arm and brought it down hard on his knee. The knife clattered onto the stone, and the assassin turned tail without a struggle and made a run for it.

"Sid," said Louise. "That dirty Sid, he tried to kill you, Johnny." She clung to him like a frightened cocker spaniel, slobbering on his chest.

"Greasy Sid, hell," said Johnny Angelo. "That was no Greasy Sid. That was a hired assassin. That man was paid to take my life."

"No," said Louise, "it was Sid. It must have been. I saw him, I know it was him."

"Nonsense," said Johnny Angelo. "I don't believe it. That man was paid to kill me."

It was the Weasel again. Plotting and hatching and scheming Johnny Angelo's downfall. And Angelo was taking no more chances. He went into hiding. He went underground to the Blue Suede Shoes and refused to come out again. He huddled in the darkness, couldn't sleep and prayed for deliverance. He was afraid to come out into the light.

He hired a bodyguard named Gattopardo. Gattopardo was 6 foot 7 inches tall and weighed 272 pounds or 19 stone and 6 pounds. He could tear apart steel chains in his bare hands. He would split a length of timber with one cut from the hardened edge of his hand. His neck was as thick as a young girl's waist.

Gattopardo wasn't vicious. He wasn't a blatant man-killer. But he was moronic, he was only half human, and he would obey any order that got through to him. Angelo took full advantage of his weakness.

He hid in the back room behind the Blue Suede Shoes, Angelo, shut in by blank walls and no windows. The doors were double-locked and Gattopardo stood endlessly outside, guarding his master. Stood without moving for hour after hour, without even shifting his feet. Angelo hid inside and knew that he was safe, but couldn't make himself believe it.

He sent out spies to trace the Weasel and eliminate him. They ranged all over town, searching, watching, asking questions. They went to every coffee bar in miles, and no one had seen him, no one even knew where he was. He had disappeared. They went back to Johnny Angelo and said that the Weasel had vanished.

He wouldn't believe it. He sent them out the next day and told them to look harder, and in the evening they returned again and said that they still hadn't found him. And still Johnny Angelo would not accept it and he sent them out again. And again and again. Until, on the fifth day, they found one of the Weasel's girl friends and asked her where the Weasel was and she wouldn't tell them. So they brought her to the headquarters of Johnny Angelo.

She was very frightened, for herself and for the Weasel.

"Why do you want to see him?" she said. "I don't trust you."

"We just want to talk to him," said Johnny Angelo. "We just want to have a friendly chat."

But the girl wasn't buying it, she swore and she wept but she wouldn't tell them where the Weasel was. Angelo made her stand and watch while Gattopardo picked up a chair and broke it into half-inch pieces.

"Please tell us," he said, earnestly. "Please don't waste out time."

"He's not here," she said. "He's gone. He's in the country. He's in another town."

He wasn't there, he hadn't been in town for months. He hadn't done it, whatever it was, it couldn't have been him. He hadn't been there to do it. The Weasel was innocent.

"Take us to him," said Johnny Angelo. "And then we can ask him for ourselves."

Because he wasn't fooled for a moment, Johnny Angelo. He realised straightaway that the Weasel was directing operations from a distance, thinking this would put him out of suspicion, thinking he would be safe that way. But he wasn't safe. He thought he could play Johnny Angelo for a sucker, but he couldn't. Angelo had it all figured out.

The girl had no choice. Angelo just pointed at Gattopardo and she led them to the Weasel. They rode in a mobike parade to another town, and through the streets in a slow black line, right through the centre and out at the other side into the slums. Along one slum street after another until they came to a house in a cul-de-sac. And up the stairway, thirteen of them, with Johnny Angelo and Catsmeat and Gattopardo and the girl herself sniffing wretchedly into her sleeve. Up three flights of stairs, narrow and cold and damp, all the way up to the attic. Johnny Angelo himself kicked the door open.

The Weasel was sitting on his bed with his feet up, reading the morning paper. The room was shabby and badly looked after; it urgently needed repainting and replastering; it was a slum. Johnny Angelo walked in first, and then Catsmeat and Gattopardo, and then the snivelling girl, and then the thirteen followers, all dressed in black leather. They all stood in a close circle around the bed. The Weasel was trapped in the middle.

The Weasel put down his paper and he looked at them. His face was pale and there were dark blue circles under his eyes.

"Well," he said. "What is it this time?"

"Questions," said Johnny Angelo. "We want to ask you some questions."

Johnny Angelo looked at Gattopardo, who stopped slouching and stood up straight, waiting for orders.

"I see," said the Weasel. "What do you want to know?"

"You've been plotting against me, haven't you?"

Angelo was calm; he was just stating facts.

"You've been trying to bring me down."

"I haven't," said the Weasel.

"You have. You've been looking for revenge."

"Revenge for what?"

"Because I beat you. Because I showed you up, because I finished you in town."

"Shit," said the Weasel.

"No shit. Fact. You tried to kill me."

"What?"

"You tried to kill me. You plotted against my life. You fixed my mobike so the engine would fail and I flunked out on Dead Man's Leap. You wanted me to die."

"No."

"Yes. You tried to run me down from a sports car, you tried to crush me to death in the open street. You tried to knife me in the back alley behind the club."

"You're nuts," said the Weasel offhand. He picked up his paper again.

"Put that paper down!" yelled Johnny Angelo. "Put it down!"

There was no calmness now, he was hysterical, he was sweating and his voice was rising higher and higher with every new word he spoke.

"It's not me who's nuts," he screeched. "It's you. You. It's you's the crazy one, you tried to kill me."

"It wasn't me."

"It was. I saw you. You tried to kill me."

"Shit."

"You tried to kill me!" Johnny Angelo screamed. "You tried to kill me!"

The Weasel waited and then he smiled at Angelo in contempt.

"Stop screaming, Angelo," he said. "You sound like a woman, d'you know that? You sound like you wet your pants. You sound like a screaming fairy."

He shouldn't have said that. He was a fool to start talking like that, attacking Angelo's masculinity. Because Angelo shut up as if his motor had been turned off. He started to stare, his eyes blind and popping in hate, but he didn't move, he didn't say a word for maybe as long as a minute. And when he did speak he was very calm, holding himself in check.

"Gattopardo," he said. "Pick up the Weasel and throw him against the wall."

And Gattopardo moved forward in obedience to carry out his orders. Like Frankenstein's monster. Like a robot, a zombie. The Weasel started to say No, but Gattopardo scooped him up in one arm and held him high in the air; the Weasel was begging and whining and screaming, and Gattopardo flung him hard head first into the wall. He crumpled like a broken egg, it seemed for a moment as if he was going to stick there. Then he slid down onto the floor.

"Again," said Johnny Angelo. And again the Weasel was lifted into the air and again he was flung head first into the wall. This time he didn't protest.

He was a busted nothing. And the thirteen followers closed in on him and gobbled him up, all of them in black leather, falling on the corpse like so many buzzards. Thirteen black vultures feasting on the carcase of the Weasel.

"Don't overdo it," Johnny Angelo said. "Easy, take it easy. Don't kill him, I don't want him killed. I wouldn't want the Weasel killed."

That was all.

PART THREE
IN THE ROCK 'N' ROLL LEGEND
OF JOHNNY ANGELO

15 The Conference

Johnny Angelo was sitting in a blacked-out room. The curtains were drawn and tied together, and there was just one floor light burning low in a corner. It was dark, gloomy. Angelo was sitting in an armchair, sipping beer through a straw, and he was playing with a Siamese cat, holding it up by its tail and twisting. Opposite him, on the sofa, were three journalists, all nervous, all sitting forward with their knees clamped tight together, all posing their heads at an identical angle. Chorus in a comic opera.

On the floor: torn newspaper, discarded beer cans, old sweaters, socks, music manuscripts strewn around. The room was a shambles.

Johnny Angelo was wearing knee-length white socks with a red rim, white T-shirt, blue girl's knickers. That was all. He was six foot and half an inch, twenty-four years of age, had shoulder-length black hair. Tall, dark and handsome. Terrible and tender. "Gentlemen?"

"Mr Angelo: quote on your new record, please."

"It's great to see it in the charts," said Johnny Angelo. "And that's where it should be, that's where it deserves to be. I'd like to thank all the faithful fans who put it there."

"And how is your tour going?"

"Great business. Just great business. This is the chance I have been waiting for—the chance to go out into the nation and let my fans see me. I felt I had to repay them as best I could for all their very wonderful loyalty to me."

Sound of pens scribbling and scratching in the dark, quiet room. Johnny Angelo was swinging in his chair, balancing on one chair leg, sipping beer and intoning, pontificating. His voice was as monotonous as a religious chant.

"Have you any amusing incidents you could tell us about the tour?"

"Just one, so far," he said, "that I recall. One night, after I did my show, a young girl came round to the stage door and

asked to see me. Now I always try to see my fans whenever at
all possible, I make it my responsibility. So I told them to send
her in, and in came this girl and it turned out she was only
maybe eight years old, I guess, just a kid, and she was clutching a teddy bear in her two arms. And up she stepped to me,
as bold as brass, and she said to me, Johnny, she said, please
will you give my teddy a kiss, she said, 'cos teddy wants to
marry you. Gentlemen,'' said Johnny Angelo, ''don't you
think that's just the cutest thing?''

Another pause. ''Mr Angelo, there has been some talk that
your popularity has begun to slide. Have you any comment on
that?''

Angelo took his time. He took his straw very slowly out of
his mouth and he shifted his position and he uncrossed and
then recrossed his legs. ''Who said that?'' he said gently.
''Who's been saying that? You better tell them to take it easy,
I believe, you better tell them to take a nice long holiday or
something. Because it seems to me they must be overworking,
they must be suffering from acute nervous strain. I mean it
seems to me they must be heading for the nuthatch, saying
things like that. You understand?''

''Sir Aubrey Challenor, Conservative Member of Parliament, has been quoted as saying that you are a dubious
influence on teenage morals. What is your reaction to that?''

''My reaction is that Sir Aubrey Challenor is well known and
notorious everywhere for a bigoted fool. This man has systematically tried to blacken my name and hinder my career ever
since I first became a public figure. He has used my position of
helplessness to spread filth and slander my name, knowing
that I am in no position to fight back. But it is my belief that he
has now gone beyond the bounds that I can tolerate and I do
not intend to let him continue without a struggle. You may
quote me on that, gentlemen.''

''How would you describe the state of your current popularity?''

''Astronomical, baby,'' said Johnny Angelo. ''Just astronomical.'' He was swinging his cat in slow wide circles, it was
hanging head downwards and purring sweetly at every slow
swing. ''When I first opened up my mouth to sing I was the
biggest thing ever to hit your scene. And in five years from
now, if I so choose, it will be still exactly the same story.'' He
let the cat's tail slip softly out of his hand in the middle of a

swing; the cat twisted as it fell, landed safely on its feet and slunk silently away. Johnny Angelo's hand continued to swing. "Gentlemen," he said. "Gentlemen, have you got all that?"

"Yes, Mr Angelo. What are your feelings about your fans, please?"

"My fans are the only good reason for me to stay in show business. Ever since I first started to make good, everyone's been trying without exception to get smart about me, to put me down in the newspapers, and to blacken my name as an entertainer before my public. They've been trying to sabotage my whole career, these so-called guardians of the public morality. But my fans have gone right on sticking by me through thick and thin, and have finally proved to everyone that Johnny Angelo could not be disregarded."

"How would you describe your stage act?"

"Entertainment plus," Angelo said. "It's bonanza and it's a thousand nights of Arabia rolled in one. I put over dream worlds larger and more exciting than real life. I provide, and you may quote me on this, a fulfilment of fantasy."

Fulfilment of fantasy. His hands were still moving in great slow swings, back and forwards like a pendulum. The three journalists couldn't take their eyes off them. "What is your appeal to the girl fans?"

"What do you mean, What is my appeal?" Angelo yawned. "I would call that a really meaningless inane question. What is my appeal? I guess they like my singing. I guess they must think I'm kind of good-looking."

Confusion: "Yes, I mean, what exactly do they see in you? No, I mean... what fantasy precisely would you say you fulfilled?"

And Angelo yawned again, swinging his hands. "I fuck. You want it straight; that's what I do. I fuck. I go out on stage and I do all the wild, brutal, really far-out things all the boys would secretly like to do to their girls, and all the girls, you see what I mean, would secretly like to get done to them. Like if the guy ever really did try it on, or even anything remotely like it, of course the girl would flip her mind and the guy would probably wind up in court. But me, because I'm way up on stage and I'm such a big star name, they let me do it to them, do you understand, and they want me to do it. It's the remoteness I get from being up on stage. And they go to see me give

them the kind of a fuck they'll never ever get in their whole
lives, a great day-of-judgement fuck. Do you understand that?
Can you see that?''

"Is that obscene?''

"That is not obscene, that is entertainment. That is an
essential social service.''

"Apart from screaming, what do the girl fans do when
you're on stage?''

"They piss on the floor. When I finish my act and the
cleaners come round to tidy up, the floor is always swimming
in piss. That's nothing: for Bobby Surf they used to pick up the
very chairs they were sitting on, break them up into little
pieces, tear off the legs with their bare hands and maul themselves. No kidding. They'd be really brutal on themselves. The
blood was sickening to behold.'' He was grinning from ear to
ear, Johnny Angelo. He lit up a long cigarette and rocked back
and up on the one leg of his chair. "They never did that for
me. Yet. They did start fingering themselves, they all do that
now. We get that far.'' He was swinging in his chair, waiting,
pausing, letting it all sink in. "Maybe old man Surf better look
out sharp for himself,'' said Angelo. "This is pussy Johnny
Angelo sneaking close up tight behind him.''

Another gap. Johnny Angelo picked up a toothpick off the
floor and began to chew it. Two of the journalists got up to go,
mumbling Thank you, Mr Angelo, thank you very much, and
tripping over their own feet as they went out. Angelo lifted one
hand, raised it in a kind of blessing.

"Gentlemen. Gentlemen, I thank you. Quote me as saying
that anyone who gives me bad publicity is doing nothing but
helping me and I sincerely thank him for devoting his valuable
newspaper space to me. I also hold no grude against the stup-
idity and inefficiency and downright evil that's been done to
me since I originally made my break. Finally, say that Johnny
Angelo thanks his fans for everything and is always thinking of
them.''

Grey notebooks and grey raincoats, they shuffled out, the
journalists, bludgeoned into sleepwalkers by the sheer weight
of words. Or density of humbug. It was difficult to know where
to start with Angelo, harder to know where to end.

They left. Johnny Angelo raised up his blessing hand again.

The one journalist who stayed on was given a can of luke-
warm beer and told to make himself at home. He coughed

carefully into his hand before he began. "Mr Angelo, how
would you describe yourself personally? What kind of man are
you?"

"Above all," said Johnny Angelo, "I would say that I was
sensitive. Sometimes I'd say almost too sensitive. I am like a
naked nerve in the wind and the slightest passing breeze
disturbs me."

Question: "Are you hard to get along with?"

"I am a perfectionist." He posed with his head on one side,
a cigarette smoking in his fingers. Angelo the true artist,
Angelo the enigma. "I am a professional entertainer. I am a
professional businessman, and I can't afford mistakes. The
man who works for me, therefore, must make himself infall-
ible."

He stubbed out ash briskly into the top of his beer can. "You
see," he said. "Do you understand that? O.K.? Like I have
some guy working for me. I tell him to go do something or
other for me and he shits it up. Then he's making a monkey
out of me, so I bawl him out. I tell him to go get himself
stuffed, I tell him drop dead, does that make me a monster? Is
this a ball game we're playing?"

He joined the tips of his fingers into an arch. He hooded his
eyes, he let his cigarette droop in the corner of his mouth.
"And I'm an artist," he said. "I live all the time at a maximum
nerve pitch. Naturally it makes me moody. So yes, all right, so
fine, I could be hard to get along with."

Question: "How good a singer are you?"

"Good. The best there is." He turned his head away
brusquely as if to say That's all, that's all I want to say about
it, forget it.

"In what way?"

"I have a natural voice that can sing anything—opera, folk,
pop, you name it. Jazz, Broadway musicals, spirituals. I have
range and I have flexibility."

As the journalist took that down, Johnny Angelo took time to
think. "Do you agree with that?" he asked. "Would you say
that was an honest appraisal?"

The journalist was grounded and didn't know what he ought
to say. He kept his mouth shut, scribbled in his notebook and
asked a new question. "Do you demand attention from
others?"

"I don't have to demand it," Angelo said. "I just get it. I am a magnet. I think, sincerely, I have that certain something. When I come into a room, no one can take their eyes off me. I was born to be the centre.''

He was smiling to himself. He liked being asked these serious questions and the journalist was tumbling over himself trying to get it all down. And they were sitting in this darkened room, facing each other, the journalist asking questions and Angelo telling him the answers.

It was nice. Talking about himself because he had been asked. Nice.

The door was opened very carefully and an American-styled college boy tiptoed into the middle of the room. He was as round as any man could reasonably be, and his skin looked like puff pastry and his shapeless sack of a face was topped by a dazzling albino crew-cut. Also, he had acne. Standing there in a T-shirt and tight white hipster jeans, he made Angelo laugh just by existing. ''That's Catsmeat,'' Johnny Angelo said. ''He fulfils the function of personal adviser and jester. Sit down, Catsmeat, and be quiet.''

He was eager, he was enjoying himself, Angelo. ''Ask me another question,'' he said. ''Anything you like.''

''What are your views on women?''

''My views on women are that women are shit. Big dirty lumps of shit. Women are filthy, they turn me sick into my stomach. Listen. With a man who is maybe your best friend or only an acquaintance even, nine times out of ten you will have a straight dealer, a guaranteed non-shit-giver. A regular guy and you can trust him. But Jesus, who would ever trust a woman? Who would be so crazy? In my view a woman is a two-faced creature, a wheedler and whiner and a mean twister, and the man who ever trusts a woman is consigning himself of his own free will into an eternity of damnation and burning hellfire. Plus, in addition, their bodies disgust me and the way they fuck is distasteful to me. I do not approve of the way they scream and scratch and make all that noise. I don't make a fuss like that, no man does, but a woman in that respect has no conception of dignity or self-restraint. I am a very particular person in all my personal habits, as I have told you, and this kind of hysteria is deeply distasteful to me.''

''Are you serious by nature?''

''I'd say I was very serious. Very intense. Life is a very serious thing, working to be a fulfilled artist is a serious thing.

I rarely laugh."

"I make you laugh," said Catsmeat.

"Catsmeat makes me laugh," said Johnny Angelo. "Make me laugh, Catsmeat."

Catsmeat made a face. He pulled his eyes apart with his fingertips so you could see the red veins, he jumped up and down and waved his arms. And Angelo laughed, he spluttered and choked, he slapped his thighs to show how funny it was. "Man, that Catsmeat, he is the nearest thing to a spastic. I mean like he is deformed. Man, that boy's so ugly I wake myself up laughing at him. You know what you are, Catsmeat? Do you? You're a cretin, baby, you're an A1 cretin. Do you know that?"

Catsmeat had a grin like a deathmask. "There was this real big woman in the shop this morning," he said, "in the bookstall. With real big tits and a nice wide arse, and she sees me at the counter, she looks me up and down, and she says to me… Johnny, shall I tell you what she says to me?"

"No," said Johnny Angelo. "Can't you see that I'm in conference? Can't you see that? Shheeet…" He turned back to the journalist. "Ask me another question," he said. "Ask me something else."

"Thank you," said the journalist, "but I think I already have all the material I need."

"No," said Johnny Angelo. "Ask me another question."

"How much money would you like to make?"

"Millions, man. Millions. I'm going to have all the lovely money in the world." He was laughing, Catsmeat was giggling, even the journalist was smiling politely. They were having a good time. "Another question," said Angelo.

"No really, you've been most kind, most helpful. I have everything I could possibly need."

Angelo had to let him go. The journalist had muddy brown leather shoes with round toes and the soles splitting off the uppers and he scuffed the carpet as he walked. "Jesus," said Johnny Angelo, "those shoes, they look bad. They look like they've had enough. Here, why don't you buy some new ones?" He pulled out a wad of notes from the band of his knickers and pushed them into the journalist's hand, humiliated him. "No," said the journalist, stammering, mumbling, "no really, I couldn't, I really couldn't."

"Shit," said Angelo in his beneficence, "shit. Take them.

Go on, take them. Present from Johnny Angelo.''

The journalist had to take the money. There was nothing else he could do.

Angelo opened a fresh beer can. He was too rough and the beer ran over the edge and spluttered onto his wrists and dribbled down his arm. He put the can up to his mouth and drank direct, and the beer slopped into his mouth and overflowed and splashed down onto his chin. He sucked in froth from the corners of his mouth. "Catsmeat," he said. "Catsmeat, make me laugh.''

"The man said to the woman Can I come in for coffee? Then the woman said to the man, You mean you want coffee too?''

"Yes," said Angelo, "that was quite funny.'' But he didn't laugh.

"The man drives up to the filling station in this brand new Cadillac with this beautiful blonde in the back. The man says to the attendant Fill her up. So the attendant gets out his great long hose and he gets busy round the back of the car. Then five minutes later he comes up for air and he says I did that, sir, now do you want something for the car?''

"Shit," said Angelo, "why d'you waste my time?'' He picked up a glass vase and threw it; it splintered on the wall behind Catsmeat's head. Catsmeat hid behind the sofa. "I was talking good to that reporter before you came in and fouled it. I was shooting him some good shit, before you scared him off.''

"Sorry.''

"Say you apologise.''

"I apologise.''

"That face. And those shitty stories. I couldn't blame him for running.'' Johnny Angelo began to brood. He cupped his chin in his two hands and stared at the Persian patterned carpet. His knickers had one tiny round hole in them, the shape and size of a halfpenny. His T-shirt had a printed photo of Elvis Presley (still) on the front. And his wild long hair hung past his shoulders and halfway down his back. He looked like Jesus Christ.

Silence. After about five minutes the door opened again and this time it was a sweet and pretty brunette who walked in, a busty brunette with nice legs and a smooth skin. Cute. Angelo saw her and he waved her way. "One minute," he said, "I'll be with you in one minute.'' She walked on through with no expression on her face, straight through into Angelo's bedroom. Catsmeat stuck his head up out of cover, peering round the end of the sofa, just in time to see her go. He couldn't quite stop himself from snickering.

"Catsmeat," said Johnny Angelo, "you foul everything. You turn everything sour on me. I look at you and I know I'm on my own. I know how all alone I am. You make me sick. You make me realise there's no one but myself."

But Catsmeat knew better. He knew the brooding was over, the fucking was going to start. And he rolled over onto his back on the sofa and waved his arms and his legs in the air. Or wallowed in the pillows like an overturned turtle. And squeaked.

"That chick," said Angelo. "She makes me sick. She wants me to fuck her again." He looked bored and his mouth was turned down at the corners. But he followed the brunette into his bedroom all the same. There was nothing better to do.

And Catsmeat rolled about on his back, on the sofa, saying "Angelo Angelo, Johnny Angelo, Johnny Angelo. Angelo is Angelic. Angelo is the Greatest. Johnny Angelo is the Greatest."

16 The Banquet

Johnny Angelo was now a very rich man. A very famous and powerful man. He lived in the style of a Roman emperor.

In his home he had created a banqueting hall. It was his favourite room. It was the room of a man whose power over other men was limitless. The heavy stone walls were hung with embossed shields and captured trophies, swords and spears and scimitars. The windows, high and small, were glazed with dust and cobwebs. And the ceiling was too high and too dark to be seen. It was like a huge black pit.

Down the middle of the hall there was a massive oak dining-table, battered and unpolished, clumsily balanced on a trestle. At the far end of this table, in front of the great fireplace, Johnny Angelo was sitting. Eating alone by candlelight. He sat in one tiny patch of brightness cut out of a great swamp of dark.

Johnny Angelo was Nero.

He dined alone by candlelight. He was wearing a white jerkin to below the waist, tight olive-green pants and knee-length hide boots. And his long black hair flowed loose, framing his face, and his face in the candlelight was angry and tormented. He still looked like Christ, but Jesus Christ the way Rembrandt would have painted him, all gloom and flickering shadows.

Three Great Danes, lean and hungry, were sitting in a hunting group in front of the log fire. Angelo was eating a chicken carcase in his fingers, chewing savagely through bone and meat and gristle and anything that got in his way, and he was flinging the bones to the hounds. There was a falcon perching on his left shoulder.

Gattopardo stood just inside the doorway at the far end of the hall, hovering and blinking in the gloom. Seeing him, the falcon flew from Angelo's shoulders into the darkness of the rafters, the sound of flailing wings echoing like gunshot in the quiet. The candles flickered in the draught.

Gattopardo had to cough to be noticed. He stood six foot seven inches in his socks and he had shoulders like a buffalo and the chest of a grizzly bear. With his bare hands he could bend cold steel and twist it into a lover's knot. With one blow he could smash a man's jaw to smithereens and with one shrug of his buffalo shoulders he could fling any man clear across the room.

He sat down at Johnny Angelo's left hand. And Catsmeat came and sat at Angelo's right hand. And then ten other men came and sat down at Angelo's banqueting table. This committee of twelve was Johnny Angelo's inner praesidium. They waited to be addressed by their leader.

But Johnny Angelo believed in good times. He believed in putting his servants at their ease before he talked to them. He could be a generous master.

He snapped his fingers once and the hall was suddenly full of light, a carnival of running servants in full livery. Gold and black, and red and green quarters. Light and music and colour. Fresh chicken for the guests, big goblets of red wine and bowls of fruit, and bowls of lemon water if they wished to rinse their hands. It was a full banquet, a great feasting.

Mice were skeetering under the table and chattering in the boards. The wind howled in the rafters and rattled the windows. The ceiling was hidden in darkness but the hall was blazing with clusters of coloured lights, red and gold and green lights. And Angelo called for more wine, for grapes and ripe peaches and pomegranates. For music. The Tannoy played gentle madrigals. "Music," said Johnny Angelo "ah music, music. Beautiful music." He played with the diamond rings that hung from his fingers. Listened with his head on one side, popping big black grapes in his mouth.

Music, ah music. Beautiful dreamy soggy music.

Nights of Rasputin, starring Edmund Purdom as Rasputin. "Drink," Johnny Angelo shouted, "eat and drink. Eat, drink and stuff yourselves until it makes you sick." His drunken voice boomed like cannon in the spaces of the hall and cascaded back at him from the rafters. His chin was dripping grease and there was chicken flesh clinging to his cheeks. His face was red and flushed with wine, his eyes blurred. Angelo as Nero. Johnny Angelo as a Hollywood Nero.

Yolande was mid-brown, Jamaican, with long legs and long arms and a long arched neck, and a skin so sheer and smooth it would slip right through your fingers as you touched it. She was beautiful and she was arrogant and when she looked at Angelo she bared her teeth, her big lovely even teeth that shone white in the dark.

The madrigals died down. There was a soft way-down flutter of African drums. And Yolande stood on the table, shook her hips and started to do a lazy strip. Very coolly, no bothering about her audience, or not even noticing them perhaps. As if she was... not bored exactly but unconcerned, or at least, only concerned about herself. Digging deep inside herself and giving herself all the pleasure. It was a private act which they were intruding on. That made it more exciting.

Smooth-skinned and rounded, and she was a juicy as Angelo's black grapes.

The beat began to toast, she moved it on up, she started to speed it on up, and she was tasty, yes, she was succulent. Her underwear was all in white leather, white against her brown skin, and she unhooked her bra and dropped it in their faces. Her skin was glistening with oil and she leant down and shook her breasts in Catsmeat's face and a single drop of oil slid off a nipple and fell on his plate. And he giggled so much he choked. But she ground her arse in his face, then strutted away hard and tight down the table, the African drumming an orgy by this time, a whirlwind, and she peeled away her panties, kicked them off and onto the floor, and stood upright, her back to them, not moving. And she wheeled on them fast, laughing in their faces, despising them, exposing her fur for just this one tiny split-second glimpse, then reached down behind her and picked up a half-full wine bottle. Packed it in tight between her thighs and advanced on them again, on a fat man aged about forty-five, and stood over him, her arms stretched above her head, her breasts and her hips still moving. And the fat man closed his eyes and opened up his mouth, and Yolande came in forward, and closer, closer, tipped the bottle slowly over him, controlling it with her thighs. Slowly, slowly, and then suddenly the wine poured out, gushed out, flooded into his waiting throat and overflowed, choking him, and the wine ran down his chin and neck. Everybody laughed and Yolande laughed, too, laughed at him and skipped away down the table, and the fat man tried to grab her and missed. And the drumming got softer and softer, softer, and then it died away.

She never once looked at Johnny Angelo. Never once admitted that he was there.

Angelo was waiting to speak. He poured out fresh goblets of wine and the wind howled in the wide chimney. Owls called in the night outside. Bats fluttered in the ceiling. And the falcon returned to Johnny Angelo's left shoulder. The Great Danes were whimpering in their sleep.

The twelve men waited for him to speak. They wiped away their leers, and rinsed their greasy hands, and sat up straight. Coughed discreetly in the backs of their hands. Sweated. And waited.

And Johnny Angelo, like the showman he was, let them wait. He opened his mouth but for a while he didn't speak.

"Evil forces have been plotting against me," he said at last. "I have been threatened with final disaster. Listen. I have come from nowhere to be a great star, to be the biggest star there is, in my opinion. And like all great stars I have attracted jealousy and hate. I have felt I owed it to my fans to speak my mind and to be honest with them at all times. And there have been many who have called me loudmouthed and aggressive and even mad because of this. Because they could not bear to hear the truth. Then I have always tried to give my audience full value on stage and I have thrown myself wholeheartedly into my act in order to give of my very best. And there have been many who have called me obscene and disgusting and have tried to ban me and finish my career. Because I portray truth and they could not bear to see the truth. That is the kind of thing I have been up against from the start, and I have grown used to prejudice and discrimination against me. But now this opposition has taken on a more serious look and I know that I must act against it, otherwise my career will be ruined. Allow me to explain.

"At the hub lies a concerted conspiracy of showmen and businessmen and here I may mention, principally, Sir Aubrey Challenor, who never tires of inventing lies about me. Their united aim is to finish my career and to force me to leave the business I love. Towards this end they are prepared to utilise any means whatsoever, however underhand or evil. Already they have bribed many of the most important men in the business: record managers have attempted to sabotage my sessions with bad engineers, promoters have saddled me with inadequate backing groups, or forced me to frequent unsavoury dressing-rooms, or failed to promote sufficient advertising for my personal appearances. Lawyers have tried to rig my contracts. My record company has mishandled my single releases. And the press has launched and sustained a concerted campaign to blacken my reputation with charges of obscenity and debauchery. It all adds up to a well-planned and powerful plot to seduce the teenagers from my side. And I refuse to accept this without a struggle.

"These are very dedicated men we are up against. In such cases it is possible only to fight dirt with dirt. And so, much as I hate and abhor any form of strife or jealousy, I have at last been forced to defend myself against this filth."

His voice was low, restrained, beautifully modulated. It rang out hollow in the dark room. And Angelo leant forward as he talked, and looked round the table. Urgently and persuasively, he looked from face to face. "Gentlemen," he said. "I need your help to protect me from this evil."

How?

"I have at this very moment a full team of investigators at my command, scouring the byways and subterranean alleys of the show-business world, in an effort to discover the real identities of the ringleaders. We will know more precisely what we are fighting when they have delivered their reports, but it is already clear to me that the campaign will become increasingly open and violent in the near future."

Guff. Blague. The followers of Johnny Angelo sat drunk and dazed around his banqueting-table and were smothered in words, drowned in this unending torrent of verbal diarrhoea. They stared at the wreckages of chicken in front of them, scared even to look at each other.

Johnny Angelo stood at the top of the table and didn't stop ranting. He leant forward with shining eyes and thumped the table for emphasis. Or he threw one hand into the air, his finger pointing to the sky, as if he was appealing to the blind figure of Justice.

"I have reason to believe that the next stage of their plan will involve increased physical violence. They will tempt me and bait me into losing my temper and making scenes in public places, so that I will establish the name of drunkard and brawler for myself. I need your help to prevent such incidents. It is up to you to make sure that no such scenes will come to pass. It is up to you to shield me from aggression and provocation. It is well known that I have a fast temper and cannot resist a fight. It will be your duty to save me from my opponents and from myself.

"You will, in short, become my personal bodyguard.

"Your secondary duties will involve you in a more active role, all of you. I want you to keep exact track of each of the ringleaders, once we have pinned these down. And to discover who their associates may be, and what their future designs against me are. This will be demanding work and, in any of these enterprises, I will guarantee you a commission of fifty pounds on each significant piece of new information you bring to light. This will make your work worthwhile."

Silence. The falcon stirred on Angelo's shoulder, ruffling its feathers. The moment hung.

Johnny Angelo stood tall at the end of the table, his chest pushed out and his arms thrown wide and his mane of hair flowing wild behind him. "Fuck them," he said. "Fuck them all. A dirty fuck in the eye of each and every one of them. And fuck the lot of them." He drank off his glass of wine in one swig, picked up the bottle and drank from that, drank and drank, drank until it was quite empty, and raised the empty bottle high above his head and began to swing it. He stood in the depths of his banqueting-hall, spotlit by candleglow in his biblical fury, and first he whirled the bottle slowly and then he whirled it fast, fast, faster and faster until he let it go and it flew up high and burst against the walls. The crashing glass echoed and echoed and re-echoed, filling the hall.

Jesters came in. Acrobats and jugglers and clowns. Acrobats who did handstands on the chairs and executed complicated flying somersaults across the table. Or jugglers, dressed in pierrot costumes, who threw coloured balls up high, red and yellow balls, up high into the ceiling, where they rose and fell in fountains. And moving lanterns, coloured magic lanterns. Catsmeat sat at Johnny Angelo's feet and told him jokes. Pretended to be Quasimodo, hunchback of Notre-Dame, inching round the table like a crippled crab, his hands hanging down to his ankles, one shoulder raised eight inches above the other, his face twisted into a tight little ball of evil. He came fawning to Johnny Angelo and Angelo emptied a bottle of champagne over Catsmeat's head.

Two huge Negroes with the shoulders of oxen were guarding the main door, juggling with lighted flares. They were

naked to the waist and wore skintight black pants. And the
flares ran snaking patterns on their black chests, and their
skins glistened wet with sweat and the heat, and their bunched
muscles stood up tense and hard as stones. There was no talking; they burnt themselves in silence.

Catsmeat wore a bright green shirt, decorated with stars
and suns and moons in alternate pink, puce and orange. He
followed Johnny Angelo everywhere, telling him dirty stories.

The cold hall was hot and bright with multicoloured lanterns, twirling and swinging in the wind, beautiful, and the
floor was a web of flickering reflections. And the jugglers,
acrobats, the black slaves: wonderful, wonderful. Johnny
Angelo was lifted bodily from his chair and carried to a chaise
longue that was covered in reams of golden silk. And he was
surrounded by his followers, men and women, very beautiful
women, who chattered and giggled and talked to him, who fed
him ripe peaches and brought him champagne to drink from
their slippers. Johnny Angelo was playing Emperor.

And still he had the nerve to get sorry for himself.

"All alone," he said. "Even now I am all alone."

"No," said Catsmeat, "no, Johnny, no. I'm here."

"But I don't see you," said Johnny Angelo. "I don't see any
of you. Shout!" he screamed. "Sing, get drunk, make jokes,
make love. No matter, I am on my own."

The *pièce de résistance*, Johnny Angelo's greatest master-
piece, Yolande climbed a silken rope ladder from the table
onto the largest and most central of the many massive candle-
abras that ran down the middle of the hall. Then she started to
swing from it, pedalling with her legs, and her breasts fell free
and her hair trailed out black behind her, and her body glinted
with oil and sweat in the bright light. She swung round high
above them and, when she got to Johnny Angelo, she leant
over and spat down into his eyes. He squirmed and liked it.

He rose from his couch, Johnny Angelo, reeling, and he
staggered blind over to the table and he raised high his glass.
"Fuck them," he bellowed. "Fuck them. Fuck them all. An
evil fuck in the ear of each and every one of them. Fuck them.
Fuck them. Fuck them " And again he whirled his glass above
his head, tottering against the table. And again he swung it
slow and swung it fast and faster, and sent it hurtling high and
wide and magnificent to shatter against the walls. "Fuck
them," he said again, gently this time, maudlin. "Fuck them.

Fuck them all.'' And he slumped slowly forward, unconscious,
falling across his own table.

17 The Illness

Johnny Angelo was sick.

He had migraine. His head hurt and he kept feeling dizzy.
He felt like nothing on earth.

He was sitting up in his four-poster bed, propped up on
feather-duster cushions, tenderly wrapped in lavender-scen-
ted sheets. He was wearing a white lace nightgown, decorated
with pale gold frills at the neck and cuffs. He looked pretty,
but he didn't feel it.

His doctor had already told him that it was nothing serious,
nothing that a day in bed wouldn't put right. But Angelo
wasn't used to sickness, and he was fretting like a spoiled
child of six. He shouted and he swore, he flung his cushions at
Catsmeat's head. And he had already reduced one of his
chambermaids to tears by the foulness of his language and the
pettishness of his temper. But he wasn't shouting now, he was
all burned out. He just lay and sulked.

The room was vast, painted white for peace. Four golden
Ganymedes fluttered down from the four intersections of wall
and ceiling. And a Cupid on a high stand in the middle of the
floor aimed his dart symbolically towards the bed. The white
paint was set off wherever possible with generous doses of
gilt, and the windows were covered by lace curtains of finest
spun gold. The whole conception was Johnny Angelo's
personal brainchild and he was justly proud of it.

The whole area of the ceiling was covered by one great sheet
of mirror. There was a battery of ten lights on the floor and a
remote control system of ten buttons by Angelo's bedside, so
that he could lie in bed and reach out a lazy finger, and see
himself reflected and magnified in any combination of ten

colours. When he made love, for instance.

Catsmeat was sitting at Angelo's bed. And Yolande, and Gattopardo, and the praesidium of twelve. And Johnny Angelo's personal astrologer. They were all waiting for him to speak.

But he sank down lower in his sheets, groaning. Exhausted, he let his head fall sideways onto his shoulder. He couldn't breathe, he said.

The old routine. He had to keep them waiting.

"I want to tell you a story," he said. "About my early childhood. One night when I was eight years of age, I found that I was unable to sleep. I lay awake for several hours and still I couldn't doze off, and so, exasperated at last, I got up and tiptoed down to my parents' room to ask for a glass of water. As I approached the room I heard the sound of voices raised in anger and, instead of barging right in, I crouched down and took a look through the keyhole. Gentlemen, I saw the whole scene. I heard it all. In the room were my mother and my father and my father's best friend, and they were quarrelling. I heard it all. I heard my mother say that she wanted a divorce, that she had been having an affair with my father's friend, and that she wanted to go off and get married to him. And my father wasn't saying anything, he just listened to this with a bowed head, and then, quite suddenly and without warning, he turned around towards the door and I saw his face. Gentlemen, I have never forgotten the expression of desolation and betrayal on my father's face at that moment. It is always with me.

"The sequel to the story, you may well find, is no less interesting. It occurred when I was eighteen years old and I had not seen my father for many years, I did not even know what had become of him. Then one day I got a letter from him, out of the blue, asking me to come and see him. The address he gave was in the country, so I took the train and in due course I arrived at the address given. Much to my surprise it turned out to be the largest country estate I had ever seen in my life. Clearly, my father lived somewhere in a small house on the estate, but, of course, I did not know where. So I thought the best thing for me to do was to go up to the main house and ask where I might find him. So I walked for miles up the main drive, through forests and exotic gardens, and in due course I came to a massive stone country house, and I rang on the bell. I waited for a minute or so, and then the door opened, and a man asked me what I wanted. Imagine my surprise, it was my father who had answered the door. My father owned this house and this estate and everything, the whole lot. I was too stunned to speak, I just stood there gaping, and he waited for a few seconds and then he said Yes, he said, can I help you? Could you believe it? Could you? He did not even recognise me. Me, his own son.

"I introduced myself to him and he welcomed me and led me into the most luxurious, palatial home, that was grander than my wildest dreams. It was a temple of perfection. My father was a millionaire.

"I asked him why he wanted to see me and he said Son, you are on the threshold of your manhood and I may never see you in my life again. I want you to know the lessons I have learnt through my own experiences, so that you will not repeat my mistakes. When you were a child, he said, and I was married to your mother, I had everything that any man could wish. I had love and family and stability, and I let it slip right through my fingers. And why? Because I was not prepared to defend it. Because I was a cuckold and a fool, and I did not defend myself. Your mother deserted me and ran to the arms of my best friend. I was abandoned, betrayed. And I swore that I would never be anyone's sucker in my life again. I made an oath on it, an oath that I have never broken. I have become a millionaire. I have won myself respect and wealth and the many things of beauty that surround me. Because I have held on to what was mine by rights. I have fought for it, I have defended myself at all times. I have not taken what belonged to others, I have not let them get their hands on what belonged to me. Because it was my own and no one else's. Because I worked and sweated and suffered to win what I have won. And no one else will steal it from me.

"The words of my father, my own father," said Johnny Angelo, "this father who was betrayed by my mother and who in turn betrayed me, his son, by not recognising me. I have never forgotten them. I have based my life on them.

"I am a very famous man," Johnny Angelo said, "a very rich man, a greatly idolised man. And I have not come into my fame overnight. I have had to force my way up inch by inch over the years. I have known hard days, hard weeks and months and years, days when I did not know where my next

penny was coming from and it was hard to go on believing in
my own potential. And nevertheless I have scrambled on
through all the setbacks and obstacles, I have fought my way
through, and I have reached the heights of my chosen profess-
ion. By will-power and faith and talent. I have followed exactly
the words of my father. I have carried on his heritage.

"Now these men, these conspirators, begin to plot against
me. They are jealous of me and they want to drag me down.
And there are two courses open to me, I could do one of two
things. I could accept it. I could say Yes. I could give up all
these things I have worked so hard to get, and I could go back
into obscurity and filth and poverty. I could surrender my life
to them, my life and my future. Or I could fight back, I could
hold on to what was my own. I could say No to them, No, these
are my possessions and triumphs, I won them by my own hard
labour and I will surrender them to no man. I could say that,
fight. And show them that they are not dealing with any ordin-
ary person, no weak-kneed walkover. But with Johnny Angelo.
Johnny Angelo himself.

"And which of the two courses shall I adopt? What is the
action of an honourable man?

"I shall fight back, of course. I shall defend myself. I shall
do as my father himself would have wished, remember: I have
not taken what belonged to others, he said to me, but I have
not let them get their hands on what belonged to me. And I, I
Johnny Angelo, am not defending merely myself here, but the
memory of my father, too, the memory of my dead and betrayed father. I believe in this. I believe that I can fight, and I
will fight. That I can win, and I will win. Fight and win: for
myself and for my father. For Johnny Angelo and his dead
father."

Johnny Angelo was sitting up in bed, leaning forward, his
hands were clasped tight in front of him. He choked and
couldn't go on. He had to hang his head. He had to hide the
tears that filled his eyes.

"My astrologer has told me that I am about to enter a period
of great fortune. I have considered this, I have thoroughly
mulled it over. And I have decided to act on his advice. I have
decided to fight back right now, no fuss, no delay. I have
decided to counter-attack before their plots can be carried on
any further."

It was a long speech and it wasn't finished yet. The inner

twelve were shifting about uneasily in their chairs, or crossing their feet or coughing or counting sheep or surreptitiously scratching themselves. And Johnny Angelo had to raise his hand for order. He was holding a bright red dossier.

"I must confess that so far we have been unable to work out the identities of all the conspirators. Or the exact make-up, policy and strategy of their plotting. But intuition and known facts have led us to identify several well-known personalities who would clearly be in the forefront of any activity against me. This red dossier I am holding includes all the information we have at present. Using it, I will tell you all I know. From then on the rest will be completely up to you.

"As far as we can see, there are four figures certain to be among the ringleaders. First among them stands Sir Aubrey Challenor, well-known Tory M.P., who has frequently described me publicly and in private as obscene and a public menace. Second is no less a public figure than Lord Morly, industrialist, motor magnate, who is in my view nothing but a prude, a bigot and a puritan. And he has claimed time and time again that I am corrupting the purity of British youth, and that in fact I should be locked up without delay in a mental home.

"Thirdly we come to Bobby Surf, my old buddy Surf, otherwise known as the Weasel. Surf as you and I know well is in big danger of being toppled by myself, by Johnny Angelo, in the popularity stakes. What could be more natural than him putting up a struggle, particularly as he is an old enemy of mine? And fourth and last there is Sol Cinqway, gangster, who may be doing the dirty work because he is in league with the Weasel, who has been trying to do me shit for more years than I can remember.

"Somewhere behind these men there must be a leader, the link. Co-ordinator, mastermind, tactician, theoretician— Führer, in short, and we do not yet know who or what he is. Until we have found him, we are bound to be losers for ever. No two ways about it, he has to be found, he must be, he must. You must track him and catch him. Hustle, get moving, get tough. It is your job to find him and strike him down.

"I want you to pay attention to these four men I have named, too. I want them softened up and dissuaded. I want them to drop their plans and it is your job to change their minds about me by any means you think fit. Only do not kill them. I repeat, I do not want any killing.

"That is all," he said. "You may go now."

Angelo had exhausted himself. His voice was hoarse and he wanted to go to sleep.

But still it wasn't enough; Johnny Angelo had one last trick to play. Raising himself up on the pillows, he waited until the twelve had reached the door, and then stopped them. He looked at them and made them wait, looking into the eyes of each of them in turn. He was sick, white-faced; his voice was hoarse and pitched almost too low to be audible. "Go," he said, "go now and may luck be with you all."

And even now it wasn't over. He raised himself higher and higher on the pillows, seeming to rise like Lazarus from the dead. "Remember," said Johnny Angelo, "that we have right on our side." And he fell back exhausted. His eyes closed, and slowly, slowly his head fell sideways on the sheets.

18 The Conspiracy

Did Johnny Angelo really believe that members of parliament
and motor magnates were plotting to end his career?

Impossible to be sure. Probably not.

But he did believe that someone was plotting against him.
He knew it, he sensed it. Someone was scheming and conspir-
ing to do him down, sneaking up behind him, lurking always
just over his shoulder. He knew that and had known it for
years. He had fought against it for half his life at least. He had
struggled to defend himself; and in all that time he had come
no nearer to beating and ending it than he had on the first day
he noticed it. For twelve years he had gone in fear of his life.
For twelve years he had been protected by bodyguards, but
still hadn't been able to sleep. And still it didn't stop, it went
on and grew and wouldn't ever stop.

It was getting worse now. The papers were full of vile
articles against him, lies and slander. Dirty slogans were painted on his door. Vitriolic letters arrived on his breakfast table.
Young girls weren't allowed to see his concerts. He was shut
off, isolated. He was made fun of in cartoons and that was
almost the worst of all. Through it all he came no nearer to
finding out who was responsible, who was behind it all. And
he had had enough.

He wanted results. He wanted something down on paper
and he could say There, this is the conspiracy, these are the
people I am up against. This is something tangible. He was
tired of terror. He wanted, at last, to turn the tables.

About a week after the conference round Johnny Angelo's
sickbed, one of his twelve strongmen came to him and told him
that he had unearthed a fiendish plot involving Sol Cinqway.
He had gone to Cinqway's Soho strip club and managed to spy
on him while he was explaining a plan that would utterly
destroy Johnny Angelo's career. The idea was to select twenty
Soho girls between the ages of sixteen and nineteen, and to
take them along to one of Angelo's concerts the following

week. The girls were to be seated in the front two rows and, as
soon as Johnny Angelo appeared on stage, they were to rush
him. Plenty of screaming, plenty of hysteria, and when the
police carted them out, they were to go crazy: scratching, kicking, clawing, spitting, lashing out with their handbags, the lot.
It was to be a full-scale riot.

But the day before the concert, a rumour would be leaked to
the press, warning them to expect a riot and suggesting that
they send down reporters and cameramen. And, immediately
after this, another rumour would be leaked, to the effect that
the rumour was a phony.

Then the girls, after the riot, after they'd been thrown out,
would come tearfully forward and admit that they were all
hired by Angelo to whip up hysteria, and that the whole thing
was nothing but a put-on. They were also to suggest, not in
hard facts but by implication, that Angelo had enjoyed sex
with some or all of them at one time or another, frequently
with more than one at a time.

Finally they were to give the impression that they were
scared out of their minds and wouldn't tell the whole story for
fear that Angelo might try to get some terrible revenge on
them.

"I'll deny it," said Johnny Angelo. "I'll deny the whole
thing."

And who precisely would believe him? Who would want to
take his word against the stories of these innocent young girls?
It was a perfect frame.

The room was dark and lush and there was a deep silence of
concentration. Johnny Angelo sat down and cupped his head
in his two hands. Or he paced the floor, thinking. He swore, he
sweated; nothing came.

Silence. Catsmeat, Yolande, Gattopardo the strong-man.
They sat around in the darkness and waited for Johnny Angelo
to get an idea.

It came. "Listen," he said, "it's simple. All I have to do is
ring round all the papers and tell them the truth, the whole
story. Tell them the exact, specific truth—that I have discov-
ered a criminal plot to ruin my career and reputation through a
bribery smear. I will tell them the whole thing in fullest detail.
Then it will happen exactly as forecast and I will be automati-
cally cleared. And I will at the same time walk off with a front-
page spread in every newspaper in the country. How's that?"

"What if it doesn't happen?" said Yolande. "What if there is no riot? What then?"

"Doesn't happen? No riot? But it will happen," he said, "it must. You have just heard the strongman say it will happen, what more do you want?"

"But it might not happen."

"But it will."

The strongman blushed.

And Johnny Angelo, did he really believe in it? He believed in it unquestioningly. He wanted to believe in it and he did.

"But what if they find out?" persisted Yolande. "What if Sol Cinqway's mob find out you know their plans, and call the whole thing off? There is always that chance."

Ah.

"That's true," said the strongman. "There is always that chance."

"Yes," said Johnny Angelo. "There is always that chance. I will admit that."

Angelo stood at the window and peered out through the curtains. It was raining. Housewives were running for shelter, shopping under their arms and newspaper hats held to their head. Johnny Angelo didn't see them; his eyes were glazed over. He was thinking hard. "Simple," he said, "simple. We can get round that and exploit the situation to our own advantage at the same time. If I go right ahead and ring the papers as planned, there are always two possibilities. Either Cinqway won't get wind of it and go straight on according to plan. In that case, everything is just fine. Or he finds out what's happened and cancels the whole project. In that case, we can still benefit.

"This is my suggestion: we go out and hire about twenty responsible Soho girls between the ages of sixteen and nineteen, and send them down to the concert. Get them into the front rows and give them instructions to put on a really wild, really convincing riot the moment I walk on stage. Simple. Easy.

"This covers all possible eventualities, no matter what Sol Cinqway elects to do. If his girls are there to riot, then our girls won't be needed and can slip away unnoticed. And if Cinqway opts out, our girls can let go full blast and stage a massive riot all of their very own."

Whitehall farce. Spectacular and labyrinthine and altogether too testing for Catsmeat's brain. "Yes," said Johnny Angelo, "and that isn't all. Because, of course, you know exactly what's going to happen next, don't you?"

"No," said Catsmeat.

"The journalists are going to approach our girls after the show and question them. At first the girls will be unwilling to talk but later they will come forward bravely though fearfully, and they will admit that they were hired by Sol Cinqway, the notorious Soho gangster and racketeer, for the purpose of staging a phony riot and making false allegations about me, Johnny Angelo, to the press, thereby blackening my name and ruining my future career. Broken by the tough questioning of the newspapermen, the girls will break right down and confess all."

There was no argument to that. There was nothing but stunned silence.

Angelo was looking out of his window into the rainy street. He turned back into the darkened room and shot his cuffs. And his beautiful face was shining big, white and triumphant in the gloom. "Hoist by their own petard, I believe," said Johnny Angelo smoothly, "is the technical phrase."

19 The Performance

Presenting Tonite—the DYNAMIC, the SENSATIONAL, the ATOMIC, the STRATOSPHERIC—MR EXCITEMENT and MR ENTERTAINMENT himself—JOHNNY ANGELO.

Johnny Angelo was moody in his dressing-room before the show. He couldn't settle down at all. He could never relax before he went on stage. He bit his nails.

The dressing-room was a twelve by fourteen foot cell, into which were crammed Johnny Angelo himself and his best friend Catsmeat and his bodyguard Gattopardo and his Jamaican housekeeper Yolande, and some new girl friend he had picked up some time, and his road manager and his business manager and his record manager. The walls were painted a dark and murky brown and the paint was peeling, and the plaster all along one wall had been hacked out or maybe it had just fallen out of its own accord. There was one broken mirror on the wall and one unshaded light hanging from the centre of the ceiling. There was no carpet, and only two chairs between the lot of them, and there was nowhere for Johnny Angelo to hang his clothes when he changed. The air was foul with smoke. Angelo stood back to look at it, the decaying walls and the bare floor and the seven open suitcases piled any old way, one on top of another, and his mouth curled down in wild disgust. "The insolence," he said quietly, "the sheer unadulterated nerve."

Catsmeat had bought himself a set of Chinese tubular bells which he insisted on playing twenty-four hours a day. He sat cross-legged on the floor, contemplating and tunelessly tinkling. He had learned the word Mystic and he wanted to be a mystic himself. He nodded his head sleepily from side to side as he tinkled, a snake charmed by the flute, his eyes clouded over. From time to time he started a kind of jerky erratic *raga* and wailed over the top of it, whining and droning, and his head was thrown back and his nose was pointed at the sky. He was fat American-looking college boy with a bristling crew cut and puff-pastry complexion and no mind. And he sat cross-legged and podgy on the dressing-room floor and wailed a song of praise.

Only Angelo could stop him. But Angelo was making up, too preoccupied to bother.

Johnny Angelo was sitting in front of the mirror, applying eye shadow and powder and mascara. It took him over twenty minutes to make up and, when he had finished, he didn't get up but stayed where he was and looked at his reflection. He stared and stared and went into a trance, retreating into a dream world of his own. For one full hour he sat in front of the mirror and looked at pictures of himself. Gorgeous Johnny Angelo.

Johnny Angelo was staring at himself. Gattopardo was staring into space. Yolande was painting her nails. The young girl Marie was staring at Johnny Angelo. Catsmeat was practising his tubular bells. The single light bulb was misted over by rising smoke. And there was a deep-down distant roar from the auditorium.

They have no atmosphere of any kind, dressing-rooms. No one stays in them for long enough. No one drops roots in them.

Angelo dressed for the stage in pink and white striped bell-bottom pants so tight it took him fully five minutes to get them on, and a foxfur jerkin cut loose and hanging to well below the waist. And he was hung with heavy gold monogrammed bracelets and a silver crucifix round his neck and two huge diamond earrings. For camp he pulled on schoolgirl white socks that came up almost to his knees.

He had a personal hair stylist. Angelo's coiffure preparation for the stage was a matter of fifteen minutes shock treatment with electric curlers, then twenty, twenty-five minutes intensive back combing, then trimming and resetting. Until the hair curled neatly round the neck and ears instead of hanging lank and ugly straight down the back. And through all this ritual Johnny Angelo sat with surprising patience, watching the developments in his mirror. When the treatment was finished, he made his hair stylist begin again and do the whole thing over once more. It took an extra forty-five minutes.

Johnny Angelo was watching himself in the mirror, Catsmeat was still tinkling on the tubular bells. It was an obsessive sound that lulled Angelo into a deeper and deeper trance.

Johnny Angelo's shoes had regulation five-inch heels, and

his hair hung loose and flowing down his back. Magnificent: he preened himself with all the arrogance of a medieval warlord. Le Roi Soleil. Johnny Angelo, the Sun King.

The promoter came bursting in, said Johnny Angelo was an hour overdue on stage, the audience were more than restless and would he kindly get the hell out of the dressing-room. Angelo crossed his arms and stood in the middle of the room, refusing to budge. "I'm not going on," he said. "Not unless you double my fee."

"You can't do that," said the promoter. "You have no grounds."

"I don't need grounds. I won't go on unless you pay me double."

"I'll sue," said the promoter.

"Then sue," said Angelo. "See where it gets you."

The promoter looked at him. He could hear the crowd baying for blood, his blood. He looked back at Angelo again and hesitated. "All right," he said. "You'll get paid."

"Now, please." Johnny Angelo stuck out his hand.

"Not now. After the show."

"Now. Or I don't go on."

"No," said the promoter. "No, I refuse to be blackmailed."

"Gattopardo," said Johnny Angelo. Gattopardo stood up. And the promoter stuck his hand in his pockets and pulled out a wad of notes and counted them off, four hundred pounds from a wad of five hundred. "Don't bother counting," said Johnny Angelo. "Just hand me the roll."

Johnny Angelo. Warlord. Bandit King. He held up the banknotes to the light and they were for real. He turned to his reflection in the mirror and winked.

Tinkle tinkle. Catsmeat was still playing the bells.

And five thousand girls under the age of eighteen were crouching in the dark, facing the light, and howling.

The screaming had no contours, no rise and fall. It was one solid wall of sound: ANGELO ANGELO ANGELO ANGELO ANGELO. The compère was running demented up and down the front of the stage, trying to tell a joke, a blue joke, and no one would hear him out. He cupped his hands round his mouth and shouted, but no one could hear a single word. He was pelted with jelly babies and hairclips and cigarette packets and rolled-up programmes: ANGELO ANGELO ANGELO. JOHNNY ANGELO.

ANGELO ANGELO ANGELO: the compère rushed out towards the wings, gesticulating, pleading, rolling his eyes. The same thing happened to him every night of his life, but he pretended to be offended, he laid on the agony. He drew it out —ANGELO ANGELO ANGELO—and he wouldn't get off the stage. His story had been running on for seven minutes, seven and a half minutes, and the girls were writhing, in real pain, waiting for Angelo to be let loose on them.

ANGELO. The compère walked right off the stage and the screaming reared up even wilder. But still the curtains didn't part. One minute passed, two, then three minutes, and still there was no sign of action. The girls were finally being driven crazy. It was cruel, it was like stringing them up over a fire until they gradually roasted to death. ANGELO OH ANGELO OH ANGELO OOOHHH. And the compère ran back on stage and yelled the name Angelo, Angelo, Johnny Angelo: and it was drowned out in screaming, the girls wouldn't let him say it and they pelted him again, they hurled pennies and stiletto heels and any metal that came to hand, and they drove him off stage again. But he wouldn't let them off the hook, he wouldn't allow the curtains to part; he had to make them burn, it was his job, and he returned again, this time with a cardboard placard. The big word JOHNNY was written on it. JOHNNY, it said. And they screamed back JOHNNY JOHNNY JOHNNY. JOHNNY ANGELO. JOHNNY ANGELO. The screaming exploded and he ducked under shellfire and made a blind run for it. No Angelo. No sign of Johnny Angelo, and the girls were howling, baying. Baying for blood. In the dark they were already pissing in their pants, panting, sweating, shaking, and the agony wouldn't break, it went on and on and way up past breaking point and still it wouldn't give. The girls were writhing and spitting as if they had itching powder in their drawers, and the compère returned with another placard and this time he just stood there, hiding the writing, and another minute passed, two minutes, and then finally, finally he did show it and ANGELO it said. ANGELO ANGELO. AAANNGELLLOOO.

JOHNNY ANGELO.

He made his entrance.

Angelo emerging from the wings was like Marilyn Monroe running for a bus. His head was tucked coyly into his shoulder and his hands flapped up and down against his chest as he ran and his steps were taken as if he was held in by the tightest imaginable of tight, tight skirts. Camp. He pouted, he fluttered his eyelashes, he blew kisses from the front of the stage. And before he started to sing, he turned his back on the audience and daintily wagged his arse at them.

The girls were laughing and screaming at the same time, they were sitting far forward in their seats with their knees drawn up in the air and their feet thrashing and kicking, and they held their hands to their mouths, and screamed and screamed.

Johnny Angelo started to sing, he started to wail some kind of fast beat number and no one knew what it was above the screaming but they knew it was fast from the way he moved, the way his groin twitched and his head lashed round from side to side, his hair tumbling down on his chest and his hips moving up and back like a seasick roller-coaster.

And somewhere in the shadows behind him there was a twelve-piece JOHNNY ANGELO ORCHESTRA, decked out in shiny gold sequin jackets and black velvet lapels and trimming, and each uniform had JOHNNY ANGELO written on the back in big red letters that glowed in the dark. And they had their volume turned way up high, as high as it would go, the guitarists were thrashing wildly on the strings, the trumpeters were pointing their horns at the ceiling and letting fly. But nothing, no one could hear a single note above the screaming.

Angelo. He ran his hand way down the inside of his thigh and tickled himself with long lazy fingers. He pouted, he winked. He flung his arms out wide like an opera singer, prima donna, and he kissed his fingers to the audience. He danced and he minced and he switched his hips staggering as if emotion was overcoming him. He did Mr Pitiful and Sexy Ways and Night Train, and he fell to the floor, grovelling and choking in the dust, thrashing on the floor and then his hips rose up and over and he raised himself hips first into the air, and his foxfur jerkin was torn at the shoulder, the girls saw white flesh and Johnny Angelo smiled at them. Or he sang a slow, slow ballad and picked rose petals from his breast to cast them into the front tow. And he leered and he scowled, he ground his groin and every girl and poor defenceless virgin in the world was broken, he beat them and he whipped them, he kicked them in the crutch and ground them underfoot and fucked them till they fainted. "OOOOHH," he said. How

exciting! How delicious! How exquisitely naughty! And he
rushed to the front of the stage and threatened to hurl himself
into the audience and the girls rose up like wolves to devour
him.

"Try to touch me," he shouted. "Try to touch me."

"Touch me," said Johnny Angelo. "Come on. Try to touch
me."

The girls got up in their seats and rushed the stage, and
Angelo was stretching out his hands to them, calling them on.
"Come on," he said. "Come on." A line of forty policemen
stretched right across the front of the stage to protect him, a
human barrier, but they wavered under the impact of attack
and almost gave way, and one girl got up to fall slobbering on
the shoe Angelo extended to her. Before he kicked her, right in
the face, and she fell back. Maniac, madman. He would have
liked to kill them. And he soared, he pulled up his jerkin to
expose his belly and sweat fell off him in a sheet and he
scratched himself, he scratched his navel and his belly, he was
scratching at himself like a monkey. His hair hung long in
great drenched rat's tails, plastered together with sweat, and
his face was twisted with effort, his body shuddered and
caved. The stratospheric Johnny Angelo.

Please Please Please he sang, and Cry Baby by Garnet
Mimms, and One Monkey Don't Stop No Show by Joe Tex,
and he ran across the stage on tiptoe, leaping high and minc-
ing, camp, or he stood still and bent down very slowly to pick
up a yellow jelly baby off the floor, and he examined it without
moving for two minutes while the riot raged all around him,
not looking up, not moving. He put his hands up to shade his
eyes against the glare and began to move again but slowly,
very slowly like a man in a slow-motion dream or swimming
underwater or under hypnosis.

Then a gilt bracelet hit him full on the mouth. He blinked
and came back to life again. Exploded and fucked them.
Fucked them, fucked them all. "Am I delicious?" he screamed. "Am I exquisite?" He fucked them viciously. "Am I
angelic?" That was too much, that was the last straw. The
girls got up baying again and charged the stage again, their
white teeth showing and their eyes glowing red. They stormed
and this time the line of police couldn't hold them, nothing
could have held them, they inched through and wriggled
through and then they surged through, poured up in their

hundreds onto the stage and the curtain came down too late, much too late; Johnny Angelo was running for his life. Locked himself in the dressing-room and the girls were right behind him and they started to break the door down and the police could do nothing to stop them. So they hammered and howled and if they had only got through they would have torn him into tiny pieces, they would have mauled him unrecognisable, they would have destroyed every last trace of him. Johnny Angelo cowered in the corner of his dressing-room and watched the door begin to cringe beneath their fists.

In the auditorium, one of the girls was crying in the arms of her boy friend. She had got up and flung her shoe at Angelo running away; it had hit a policeman, and when her boy friend tried to calm her, she spat at him, she tried to scratch his eyes out. Now Angelo was gone and she subsided and cried her heart out. Her face lost all its shape and her mascara ran in black streaks down her cheeks and her powder got clogged into tiny ugly pink rolls below her eyes and around her mouth. Her mouth fell away and her cheeks came away from the bone, her face lost all shape, and she cried in her lover's arms like a child who saw a witch in the dark and screamed and screamed until the light went on.

All because of Angelo.

It wasn't over. The door began to shudder, it hung loose on its hinges; and the girls tried again, it creaked and it groaned and it finally gave way before them. Angelo turned chicken and made a run for it. The door caved in and the girls swarmed in just as Angelo's arse disappeared through the back window.

Angelo ran like hell and finally hurled himself sweating and swearing and shaking into the shelter of a police car. They rode him out of there with girls clinging on the back and riding the roof and fighting and screaming and clawing at his face in the window. The Johnny Angelo Show. "Some show," he said. In the history of mankind there was never a show to equal it. Never.

"The greatest," Johnny Angelo said. "The absolute greatest." And he passed out in the back seat of the police car.

20 The Buttons

This is what happened to Sir Aubrey Challenor.

"It will not be easy," he said. "Neither for you nor for me. Nor for any of us. But it is, I say, a challenge that must not and cannot be avoided. A challenge that *will* not be avoided. For, unless we are able to face up fairly and squarely to the fresh responsibilities of our age, unless we can renew and remodernise our ways of thinking, unless we can rediscover the heritage which is ours, we must inevitably fall from the forefront of world leadership, and thus, from the position in international estimation we have for so long and so gloriously held."

His microphone failed. He carried on for two more sentences, mouthing like a goldfish in a glass tank, and then gave it up. The wind howled in across the square, gathering speed as it came, making his hair stand on end and his nose run. And the rain lashed into his face, blinding him. In the square below, men stood around in their heavy winter overcoats, their collars turned up as far as they would go, stamping their boots on the stone to keep their feet warm. Sir Aubrey could hear them booing and setting up a slow handclap for him. And he wished that he had stayed in bed.

His hands were red and numb with cold and he could hardly turn over the pages of his script. His voice was hoarse and painful with shouting against the wind. The rain trickled slowly down the back of his neck. When he reached tentatively into his pocket for a handkerchief, his notes slipped from his hands, blew away before he could save them, and went straight into the chairman's face. Schoolboy farce again.

Gattopardo and Catsmeat were strategically placed right at the very front of the crush, dead centre and perhaps five yards away from Sir Aubrey himself. Gattopardo was impassive. He stood in the rain and watched the stage, waiting for orders. Catsmeat was wearing a double-lined winter coat, a big hood with woolly earmuffs, and thick blue woolly gloves. There were black inkstains on his cheek, cakecrumbs round the corners of his mouth, and three bottles of fizzy Coca-Cola slurping round in his belly. Earmuffs and thick blue woolly gloves: he looked twelve years old.

And Sir Aubrey. A fat man in his middle fifties. He had white hair and a red face, entombed in a corset-like black waistcoat. He was wearing a black suit with a thin grey stripe which had cost him seventy guineas and would now be a complete write-off. And for bravado he had stuck a grey silk handkerchief in his breast pocket. He was crouching over the dead microphone, the rain and wind were catching him full in the face, his nose was dripping uncontrollably and he could no longer feel his fingers. But in all his troubles he kept smiling a weak and watery, helpless, appeasing smile at no one in parti-cular. Getting him nowhere.

He had started with an audience of ninety-four and now he was down to fifty-eight, and, of those fifty-eight, nine were on the platform, fourteen were journalists, eleven were standees waiting at the back with boos and eggs and rotten oranges, and two were Catsmeat and Gattopardo. Subtracting thirty-six from fifty-eight leaves what? Twenty-two.

At the end of five minutes, he was able to begin speaking again. "Let us stride out together," he said. He shouted into the microphone against the wind. "Let us put our shoulders to the wheel, let us give unstintingly of our blood and sweat. Let us recall with pride those heroic days of 1940 when, even in the darkest hours of our despair, we fought shoulder to shoulder and side by side, united by a common cause, sparing never a thought for our own individual suffering, but committed entirely to the defence of our principles and of the country we all held so dear. Let us honour the example of those men and let us uphold their heritage today. Let us remember the glory of our past and let us ensure that our future will be just as notable in the annals of history. Let us march together once again as brothers and let us once again recall our motto in those days of death and glory: they shall not pass. They shall not pass." He paused and he raised one arm high into the air, letting it all sink in, letting the moment stretch. "Friends. Friends, let us stand firm."

He held it there for just one second, his arm held high and his chest expanded until his waistcoat was near to bursting. And then, in a gesture of humility, he bowed his head and his upraised hand fell slowly forward in a vague motion of blessing. Cameras clicked. The faithful twenty-two applauded in the rain.

"Now," said Catsmeat. "Do it now."

Gattopardo lumbered forward and shuffled and bulldozed up onto the platform. The thin cordon of guards was swept aside like a row of matchsticks; he swung them away in one great sweep of his arm, and he was through them and closing on Sir Aubrey. His huge gorilla body crushed down. There was a long sharp knife glinting in his hand.

Sir Aubrey jumped backwards, squeaking, squealing like a stuck pig, cringing and looking desperately for shelter. But Gattopardo gave him no chance, no time to think. He picked him up and he shook him, and he lifted up his jacket and he ripped off the buttons of his waistcoat.

Gattopardo's knife hand came up slowly, methodically and almost quietly he razor-slashed Sir Aubrey's bright pink braces.

What happened? Nothing much. Nothing very spectacular. The cameras were ready and humming. Sir Aubrey's black trousers with the thin grey pinstripes slid gently past his knees and collapsed in a heap.

21 The Scarecrow

This is what happened to Lord Morly.

Lord Morly, at seventy-nine years of age, was sitting in a wheelchair, his back to the window. He sat in the shadow and the curtains were kept drawn. Sat in his conservatory, a high oblong room, painted white. And all the furniture had been taken out and the carpets had been rolled up and removed. He was sitting in an empty room, in a wheelchair, with a tartan rug over his knees, waiting for it to get dark. He was dying of cancer.

He was no longer trying to keep himself alive. He always sat in shadow, in the half-darkness, so that no one could quite see the full greyness of his face, or the way in which his skin had become drawn like parchment, or the way in which his body had become so grotesquely wasted. He was very vain, very tiresome. The whole room was filled with the feeling of his decaying flesh, and his face had already formed itself into a deathmask.

Sometimes he received visitors and sometimes he allowed himself to be read to—the daily papers or his company statements. But on sufferance only. Normally he sat alone. He was wheeled from his bed to the conservatory at nine-thirty in the morning, and he remained there until the sun went in and the air got cold again. He had the windows shuttered to protect himself from the sun. He hid from it. He hated the sun, but still he had the door left open so that he could see the light when it sat on his threshold. And he could watch it shrink until it disappeared.

He was very still. He was deeply shrunk inside himself. It was a strange thing to watch this bent, motionless, decaying figure huddled in a wheelchair for hour after hour without moving.

He was thinking. He was thinking out the problems of his age. He was contemplating the moral decay of his time and he was formulating correct answers. He felt that the time was

right for decisive action. It was more and more obvious with
every day that his civilisation and his heritage were falling
apart. He regarded it as his responsibility to put them back
together again.

He forced himself on no one. He emerged to speak only
when his opinion had been sincerely and earnestly sought
after. Like a witch doctor, a Buddhist hermit. He sat and he
waited. He passed judgement when consulted.

This he believed to be true: that without values a civilisation
will founder and disintegrate; that the emergent generations
of Europe and America had entirely forgotten the real roots of
life; that they were being systematically corrupted by the
values of advertising, of pop, of violence and sex in cinema
and television. It was, it still is, a godless and amoral, brutal,
mindless age, and Lord Morly was waiting to put it right.

The night before, he had been on national television, putting people right, correcting their false impressions.

This morning he was sitting in his conservatory, well wrapped in rugs against the morning chill. He was sitting in his
wheelchair and he asked to be read the morning papers, listening carefully to the reports of his speech. ''Lord Morly, a
world-famous supermarket tycoon and motor magnate, last
night launched a sensational television attack on today's pop
singers. Watched by millions of viewers all over the country,
Lord Morly made his attack in a face-to-face confrontation with
a teenage panel on the programme 'Platform'. And bearing
the brunt of his criticisms was current idol Johnny Angelo,
whose wild stage antics have provoked widespread contro-
versy in recent months. 'I can regard Angelo and his like only
as cynical exploiters of the young,' said 79-year-old Lord
Morly. 'Anyone witnessing his performances might be for-
given for dismissing him as an obscene and mindless moron.
But he is not mindless—he is, in fact, a sophisticated and
intelligent businessman who is deliberately milking his teenage fans for every penny he can get. Not only this, but he is
quite consciously corrupting his audience with the filthy and
degrading displays of sexuality he so excels in on stage. It is
my firm opinion that Angelo is a menace to the moral safety of
the country, and that his mentality would be more suited to a
mental hospital.'

''Lord Morly went on to say that it was the antics of Johnny
Angelo and his sort that showed up the full religious and moral

decline of our age. Many might think, he continued, that his remarks about Angelo were overstated and indeed libellous. But he was not afraid of any legal action that might be brought against him. In fact, he would welcome it as a further opportunity to publicise his views.

"Lord Morly was making one of his now infrequent excursions from retirement. Reputed to be one of the richest men in the country, he has for years been an outspoken critic of teenage trends and morals.

"Footnote: at his home last night, Johnny Angelo said, 'This is simply further evidence that Lord Morly is nothing but a senile old fool. This is typical of the nonsense he has talked for years and I regard it as beneath me to argue back. In fact, I pity him.' "

One hundred and forty-three telegrams had arrived already, one hundred and four of congratulation and the other thirty-nine of abuse. Lord Morly read none of them. He had buried himself deep in himself again, and he didn't want to speak to anyone.

He was sitting in his wheelchair and he was thinking. And occasionally he would pick out one or other of the papers and reconsider his remarks. He was gently satisfied.

At eleven, this morning and every morning, a maid in a black and white starched uniform brought him a glass of natural orange. She wore thick black stockings and a white nurse's cap, and she was even quite pretty. But her face was raw and red and she was embarrassed in Lord Morly's presence. She was painfully scared.

He had given her instructions to curtsey on entering and again on leaving. He was an ogre. He made her weep. He never even noticed her. He never looked into her face. His face was gaunt and his body shrunken, and she hated to be near him.

He dismissed her by raising one hand from the tartan rug and touching his temple with one fingertip. He didn't speak or look at her. He did not wish to be disturbed. And his hand hung like a claw, thin and twisted and mottled, something dry and wizened like a premature baby, an ugly foetus. It fluttered in the shadow.

He sat in the shadow with his hands folded on his lap and his eyes closed. He was old twenty years beyond his age, suspended in time, and his life didn't move forward or back, it hung, and nothing moved within him or around him. Nothing penetrated, nothing disturbed him, rearranged him in any way. He was shrouded in a deep, deep calm.

He watched a daddy-long-legs inch towards him across the marble floor. The marble floor was a rosy grey. He watched his hands lying in his lap. He watched the sunlight on the threshold. At about twenty minutes to twelve his head fell forward onto his chest and he went into a doze.

His hair was short and scruffy and curiously transparent. His skull showed through it, pink showed through the white. And thick blue veins showed through the dark grey, near black, of his nose. Short-sighted, shrivelled, pedantic. He looked like a Victorian cartoon, the miser counting out his money bags. His hands were long and thin and bony, spread on his lap like the hands of a ghost.

The door opened. There were tiptoe footsteps behind him. Lord Morly was still asleep.

Someone was standing behind him. Someone was looking at him while he was asleep. He was nothing but a skinny sack of bones, sleeping in the half-dark, his hands trailing down like claws to the marble floor. He could have been a great, sinister, sleeping bird. A condor.

Lord Morly was woken by a very big hand placed roughly and suddenly and without warning over his mouth. An arm under his armpit lifted him bodily out of his chair and dumped him hard on the marble floor. Two fingers of the big hand fluttered in front of his face and tweaked his nose.

There were two men in masks in Lord Morly's conservatory. One of them, the one who had tweaked his nose, was almost a giant, and the other was almost a dwarf. Lord Morly, believing that they had come to assassinate him, sat on the floor and closed his eyes and waited for them to get on with it. But death doesn't come so easily. The big man picked Lord Morly up from the floor again and held him high in the air by the scruff of his neck so that he was hanging helpless like a puppet without strings. The dwarf began to undress him in mid-air. He was stripped of his dressing-gown and pyjamas and bedsocks and then even of his spectacles, then he was dropped, to crawl around naked on the floor.

His arms and his legs were like twigs, and the empty sack of his belly hung down low, almost covering his genitals.

The dwarf produced a lifesize scarecrow and began to dress

it in Lord Morly's dressing-gown and bedsocks and pyjamas
and glasses. And, not without trouble, the giant and the dwarf
managed to get the scarecrow sitting securely in Lord Morly's
wheelchair. At this point the dwarf began to giggle behind his
mask.

They went. They tiptoed out into the garden, and left Lord
Morly there to be found by his servants.

This was the product of Johnny Angelo's imagination. Lord
Morly lay naked, grotesque on the floor, whimpering for help.
And the scarecrow sat impassively in the wheelchair and
watched him.

22 The Park

Johnny Angelo was restless.

He stood at the window. He peered out from behind his curtains and it was pelting with rain. There were huddles of schoolgirls everywhere, standing in the rain, watching his window, waiting, waiting. They were soaked to the skin and still waiting. They had been there since nine o'clock in the morning and they would still be there at six in the night. All they wanted was to see the curtain move and know that Johnny Angelo's hand was holding it. Or to see his shadow shifting in the upstairs room. Anything that was him. Anything at all.

They loved him, they adored him, they worshipped him. They were his, they belonged to him and he owned them. They would even stand out in the pouring rain for him, hour after hour, in the hope that his curtain would move: what more did he want?

He was still restless.

It was raining hard. Johnny Angelo saw the pretty secretaries run past his window on their way to lunch, their hair blown out of place by the wind, their stockings spattered to the knee with mud. They went running past in twos and threes, going as hard as they could for shelter, and they were shouting, giggling, holding up newspapers to their heads to keep them from the wet, and they never once looked at his window. They didn't even know he was there, but he owned them just the same, they belonged to him. They were his.

Still he was sick. Still he was restless.

He was depressed at the way things were going. He was finally sick and tired of the fussing and the fighting, the plotting and the counterplotting; he was sick of it and he wanted to stop. Twenty-five years of non-stop hustling, hysteria, and he had had enough. It wasn't getting him anywhere. He was stuck; he felt as if he was back exactly where he started.

It was serious. It was the first time in his life that he had ever reviewed himself. It was the first time that he had ever

imagined things being conceivably different. He felt uneasy
and dissatisfied, and he wondered why.

He watched the girls from behind his curtain: they stood out
in the rain, and they waited and waited for him to show himself. But he didn't. He remained in hiding.

Enemies. He had had so many and he had lost count of
them, the opponents he had struggled with and defeated and
humiliated. And for each one he had beaten, there had always
been a fresh one to take his place. So that now Johnny Angelo
was no nearer to the finish of it than he had been on the day of
his birth. And he could see no possible end to it.

Catsmeat and Gattopardo, his followers, were out at that
very moment, waiting for someone, or following them, or even
beating them up. Obeying Johnny Angelo's orders.

Who? Which one this time? Bobby Surf, alias the Weasel,
downed three times already and still coming back for more? Or
Sol Cinqway? Johnny Angelo didn't know. There were too
many to remember, too many faces and too many names, too
many ways of dealing with them. And Johnny Angelo had
forgotten.

Sir Aubrey Challenor. Lord Morly. Two beautiful operations, two enterprises planned to perfection. Each of them the
last word, the finishing punch, the one and only gesture
guaranteed to burn them off for ever. And Angelo wasn't
pleased. He was indifferent, he was bored by the whole thing.
He hardly smiled.

It was ashes, all of it. He hated it, hated it, he wanted out.

And why not? Why not quit, give the whole thing up?

Because it was too late. He was committed. It had become
his life. And because it wasn't that easy, THEY wouldn't let
him, THEY wouldn't stop plotting just because he stopped
retaliating, THEY would go on and on for ever. And Johnny
Angelo was fated to fight with them until the day he died. He
knew that.

It wasn't Angelo who had started it, after all. It was them.
Them, his enemies, his rivals. Who wouldn't ever give him
peace. Who wouldn't let him be

He looked out of his window again. It was still raining. The
girls were still waiting. They saw the curtain move and they
screamed: Johnny Angelo, Johnny Angelo. He looked down at
them and they were standing quite still and looking up, making no effort to shelter. They were in love with him. They all

loved him. They would have given their lives for him. And they stood in the rain and waited for the curtain to move.

At the very front of the crush, there was a young boy aged perhaps sixteen. He had long straight blond hair and it was slicked down cold and wet by the rain, hanging off his shoulders, clinging to his cheeks. And he had a snub nose and raindrops kept hanging off the end of it, not quite falling, and he tried to shake them off by nodding his head. He nodded his head because he didn't want to be crude and wipe off raindrops with the back of his hand. When Johnny Angelo might be watching.

Johnny Angelo had no friends and it was too late for him to start now. He would have liked to walk out of his front door and get into the streets, talk to that young boy and drink beer and make women with him. Take it easy for a change. He couldn't do that. He couldn't walk out of any front doors and he couldn't go walking in any streets. It was too late for that and he would only get himself torn to pieces.

The boy was standing right under his window and looking up. Johnny Angelo couldn't go himself but he sent someone out to find what his name was. The man came back and told him Arthur. "Arthur," said Johnny Angelo. "That's a nice name."

Then Johnny Angelo forgot all about him and tried to think of something else, something pleasant. He walked about his room and wouldn't be still. Sat down in his armchair, stood at the window, paced the floor. Nothing came.

He was sick. He looked out of the window. The boy was still standing there, his face turned up towards him. A fresh face, very young, very unused. It was an easy face to remember. Arthur.

It was still raining. Johnny Angelo was trying to think about the business at hand, about Gattopardo and Catsmeat and the endless conspiracy, but he couldn't concentrate. Brawling and bloodshed and anger. And terror; he couldn't remember when he hadn't been afraid. And his father and his mother and his two sisters, the teacher, and the Weasel, and Yolande and Catsmeat and shouting Elvis is the King. His gunslinger's uniform, and the cat who ate the bird, and KICK ME on his back—all crowding back on him. He didn't want to think about it.

He called his chauffeur and asked to be taken for a drive in the park.

The park was wet and miserable, and Johnny Angelo cruised through it slowly, looking through the window. Old women sat underneath the dripping trees on green benches. Kids were crouching at the edge of the pond, sailing model yachts. They were concentrating very hard, everything in them focused on getting their boats from one side of the pond to the other. That was all; it was simple. But they were so passionate, so intense about it, that Angelo couldn't believe it. "Stop the car," he said. "I want to watch."

There was a race. Three yachts across the breadth of the pond. And the three boys, the owners, were shouting and screaming, throwing sticks into the water to make the boats go faster, running in circles, straining and praying for their own boats to win. Angelo laughed.

The race was won by a yellow boat with a bright red sail. "Drive on," said Johnny Angelo. "Drive on, I want to see something else."

He cruised through the park. Rain was dribbling down the car windows; the sky was black and it was beginning to get dark. Waste, Johnny Angelo was thinking. I can't believe in so much waste.

Three teenage girls were walking across the park, short skirts and PVC macs. Beautiful, Johnny Angelo thought, they're really beautiful. They were talking to each other and kicking up the stones as they walked. He could hear them giggle; he could distinctly hear the gabble and shriek that young girls make. Sentimental Johnny Angelo, he was enchanted.

He followed them, going very slowly, looking at their legs. Some boys came past and tried to chat them but the girls just stuck their noses in the air and walked by. Johnny Angelo laughed. He rubbed his palms together and told the chauffeur to drive closer. One of the girls had taken out a packet of gum and was handing it round, and they walked on in the wet, chewing, taking it easy, leaving dark tracks across the damp grass. Johnny Angelo thought they were marvellous.

Then he overdid it. He drove up too close and the girls heard the car sneaking up behind them, turned round and saw him, only ten yards away. They didn't move for a moment, weren't sure what to do. Then they started to run towards him. They were shouting and screaming: Johnny Angelo. Johnny,

Johnny Angelo. They had seen him; they knew it was him. Johnny Angelo. They wanted to touch him.

They were hideous, their faces were huge and crude and hysterical. Faces of fans. He hated them.

He was terrified. "Drive on," he yapped. "Drive on, I don't want to talk to them.'

Run away. Cut out. It was bitter. Angelo couldn't bear to see them or be touched by them. He had had enough of all that. He was all through.

It was all a waste.

His whole life for nothing. All his life he had wanted to be a great star and now he was a great star and suddenly he didn't want to be. What was it but waste?

He drove home through the rain without a word, staring out of the window. Catsmeat and Gattopardo were waiting in his sitting-room, bursting to tell him the news. "Yes?" he said. "What is it?"

"Surf. Bobby Surf. The Weasel."

Bobby Surf. The Weasel. He looked at them and hesitated. He wanted to tell them to go to hell, but he didn't, he couldn't. It was too late, much too late to start turning back. He was committed, he was stuck; there was no getting away. The one word, conspiracy, had taken over his life.

He sighed a lovelorn prima donna's sigh, sat down and looked at them. He was still thinking about the three girls in the park and the yellow boat with the red sail. But what could he tell them? "Yes," he said, "I suppose you'd better tell me all about it."

23 The Final Revenge

This is what happened to Weasel Bobby Surf.

He had been drinking in the discothèque until the early hours of the morning, and he drove home with his girl, drunk and only half awake. All he wanted in the world was to get between the sheets.

He put his key into his front door lock and turned. But the door swung open of its own accord. Puzzled, he walked in, the girl behind him. And stopped. And stared. The hall was littered with torn flowers and broken glass; the flower vases had been broken one by one, and the water still showed wet on the walls and floor. And the walls had been systematically splashed with great cans of paint, green and purple paint, and the empty cans had been thrown on the floor. The hall cupboard had been kicked in. The telephone wiring had been pulled out at the roots, the instrument flung against the wall. The parquet flooring had been scored and rescored by a sharp knife, churned over until it looked like a football field. And the last dribbles of paint had spread out across the carpet in long thin tendrils, like trails of blood in a horror film.

The girl screamed and retreated into the doorway again, her hands to her mouth. Paint dripping from the doorposts stained her stockings.

Surf went on alone, switching on the light by the gaming-room door. His bodyguard Louie was laid out by the window in a pool of paint and blood, his face twisted in pain and his hands flung up to protect his face. He was unconscious. He had been coshed twice at least on the back of the head and then kicked hard in the ribs and guts. There were deep dark marks on his belly.

And the room. Behind Louie, the window had been forced open and shattered. Broken glass had been trampled and scattered all round the room. The velvet curtains were fluttering loosely over Louie's body.

Nothing had been left alone. It had been thorough, ritualistic, completely mindless. The card table had been turned upside down and the legs ripped off, the green baize ripped into shreds. The curtains, which had extended along the full length of the one wall, had been pulled down, torn up, splashed with paint, and strewn around the room. The drink cabinet had been broken in and the bottles one by one methodically smashed. Surf trod on glass with every step he took. There was a stench of spilt alcohol and mixed paint. The hi-fi had been kicked in and the speakers destroyed, the records taken out of their sleeves, broken and hurled against the walls, the sleeves carefully torn in two. Nothing had been neglected.

The armchairs had had their stuffing torn out and scattered around the room. The feathers collected in big piles in the corners. There were feathers on the walls and on the floor and in the hi-fi and in the bar. Feathers attached themselves to the bottoms of Bobby Surf's trousers as he stood and looked at Louie.

This was Johnny Angelo. This was his big idea, Angelo's own brainwave. Looting and pillaging and destruction. Violence and revenge.

All the mirrors had been smashed, and smashed again until no recognisable image remained.

Surf's sister Claudine had been knocked out and beaten up and gagged and raped in her own bedroom. She was sitting naked on her bed, her feet roped together and her hands tied behind her back. Villainy in the style of the silent movies. She was bleeding from face and breast and belly. She fell half conscious into her brother's arms when he untied her.

Claudine's room. Someone had smashed the windows. Someone had pissed on her sheets and poured wet paint on the Persian carpet. Someone had put his foot through her television screen. Someone had torn her door off its hinges and broken it into firewood with an axe. Someone had pulled the paintings off the walls and broken the frames and slashed the canvases. Someone had shattered her mirrors. And in such detail. Her clothes had been taken from her wardrobe and ripped apart. Her handkerchiefs had been cut in two. Her make-up had been spread around the room, her perfume bottles broken and her lipstick smeared all over the walls.

24 The Pretty Boy

Johnny Angelo was living the life of a hero. He lived in luxury
and he made a lot of money. He drove fast cars and he was
surrounded by doting women.

The conspiracy against him was coming under firm control.
Sol Cinqway had been foiled and Sir Aubrey Challenor's
braces had been slashed and Lord Morly had been made ridiculous and Bobby Surf had been eliminated. It didn't matter
what got thrown at him, Batman Johnny Angelo turned the
challenge back.

At any time there is always one person, one and no more,
who sums up what's going on better than anyone else and is
therefore taken up by the papers as the leader of his generation, Hollywood enlargement and projection of a whole decade,
an identikit picture of everything. And Johnny Angelo was it,
was on, played tag for his whole generation. He was the great
hero of his time.

Then a small thing happened. It was to do with Arthur.
Johnny Angelo was everything to Arthur, a godhead. Arthur
dressed like Johnny Angelo, walked and talked like him, wore
his hair the same way, sang the songs of Johnny Angelo and
was the envy of all his friends. He was sixteen years of age,
Arthur, a pretty boy who rode a motor scooter, liked Otis
Redding and Wilson Pickett, and swallowed purple hearts by
the hundredweight.

He stood outside Johnny Angelo's house every night and
asked to see him. And then one night, after waiting three
hours in the ice-cold street, he was finally admitted to
Angelo's presence. A very pretty boy of sixteen with soft blond
hair, neat bones and a snub nose.

Johnny Angelo was sitting in his most comfortable armchair, wearing a flowered Japanese silk dressing-gown. He
was drinking white wine. He was at ease, feeling unusually

relaxed. "Good evening," he said. "What is your name?"

"Arthur."

"Arthur, I like that. Arthur is a very nice name. I wish there were more people called Arthur." He stopped to sip between each phrase. He was beaming. He was at his most regally benevolent. He must have been a little bit drunk. "Well, Arthur," he said, "and why have you come to see me?"

"Because I am one of your greatest fans, sir. I have followed your career ever since you started and I have every single record you ever made."

"Every record I made? My, that's quite some collection, Arthur."

"Thank you, sir."

"No need to call me sir, Arthur, no need to be formal at all. Just talk to me like you would to any of your friends. I like to think of my fans as among my closest friends in every way and I sincerely hope and trust they feel the very same way about me. So just make yourself at home, Arthur, and don't feel restricted in any way. Imagine that you have lived here all your life. Have a glass of wine," said Johnny Angelo. "Relax and get a few drinks inside you."

Johnny Angelo was leaning on his mantelpiece, tall, beautiful, a little drunk, the perfect host. "And tell me," he said, "which record out of all the records I ever made is your own personal favourite?"

"I don't know, it's hard to say. Hurt Bug, I suppose, and maybe You Can't Get Through To Me."

"Isn't that strange?" said Johnny Angelo. "Isn't that quite extraordinary? Because those happen to be my own two greatest favourites of all time." Delighted, grinning all over his face. "Now isn't that a real coincidence?"

Arthur sat back, beginning to enjoy himself. The wine crept over him. "Like the wine, Arthur?" said Angelo.

"Yes, sir. I like it very much, sir, thank you."

"Not sir, Arthur," said Johnny Angelo. Wagging his finger at him, cocking his head to one side coquettishly. "And I'm glad you like the wine because it is my own favourite. I have special consignments flown over regularly from the vineyard itself, direct from France. I believe that with wine, as with everything else, only the very best is good enough."

Arthur didn't know about wine. He rode a motor scooter and took pep pills, and wine wasn't his territory at all. He was only a very young boy, very simple-thinking and greatly overawed. "Listen, Arthur," said Johnny Angelo. "If you are interested, why don't I take you around my house and show you a few of the little things I've bought? How would you like that?"

"I would like it very much. Thank you," he said politely.

At the top of the stairs there was a Dutch painting which Johnny Angelo had bought as a Rembrandt. "This painting is by Rembrandt," he said. "Rembrandt is the greatest painter in the world. He lived in Holland in the Middle Ages and his paintings are the most expensive of all because everyone realises that they're the best.

"This is a painting by Degas, out of the Impressionist school of France. Degas is recognised as one of the all-time great old masters and this is my most favourite of all his masterpieces. To me, this is purely poetry in motion and colour—no shit, I count myself as privileged to live with such things of beauty.

"Here we have a very famous statue by Rodin, who was also French out of the Impressionist school, called The Kiss." Johnny Angelo stopped in front of it, delicately sipping wine, drinking in the beauty of it. He patted the man's rump appreciatively. "Out of the ugly, the beautiful," he said. "That is the secret of all great art—look into the hideous and see beauty that you and I are not capable of seeing. The Kiss, by Auguste Rodin. A very lovely and sublime work of art.

"I need beauty like most people need water. I cannot bear ugliness, Arthur. I cannot bear filth and squalor and depravity. I cannot abide meanness or sneakiness in any way. I am a very fastidious person in my life, believe me, and dirt makes me physically sick to see."

Johnny Angelo was getting garrulous. He was sitting in his armchair with his feet up and the colours of his dressing-gown were as radiant as a peacock's fan. "Beauty," he said. "Beauty. Loveliness. I surround myself with beauty. I cannot bear filth in any form. You think I like pop, I tell you I don't, I think it's vulgar, raucous. I collect the classics and study them over and over again whenever I get the opportunity. I listen to Gershwin and Sinatra and Tony Bennett, all the great musicians and quality singers of the world. I listen to them and I try to learn from them. I attempt to drink in their beauty and nourish myself on it."

The hi-fi played George Gershwin's Rhapsody in Blue. It was very loud and passionate. Johnny Angelo listened with his eyes shut, his head swaying, a faint smile around his mouth, the glass of wine swirling in his hand. The connoisseur, the aesthete. "Tell me, Arthur, what do you intend to do when you grow up?"

"I don't know."

"Well, you certainly have plenty of time in which to make up your mind and I see no reason why you should not enjoy these years of your freedom to the utmost. You are going through the richest and most rewarding years of your life and it is my opinion that you should be free to experience them without the heavy burden of responsibility."

Arthur didn't know what to make of this. He didn't know what he ought to say and he was wise enough to say nothing. Also he was half drunk already. "Tell me," said Johnny Angelo, "do you have a girl friend?"

"Not any one in particular."

"And do you like women?"

"Yes," said Arthur. "I like them all right."

"Do you? Well, to be perfectly open with you, Arthur, I cannot feel the same way. To me a woman is a creature never to be trusted, and also mentally and emotionally inferior and repulsive to me. In addition, I find their softness and fatness distasteful and I often feel that they are dirty. I cannot bear the way they are always shrieking and screaming and attempting to cause an upset: do you see what I mean by that?"

Arthur made a meaningless, noncommittal gesture of the hands.

"I mean," said Johnny Angelo, "I fuck them. Of course I fuck them, you have to fuck them, don't you? But I wouldn't say I exactly liked them, that's all.

"Listen, I believe that a woman's body is soft and flabby, where a man's body, properly cared for, is hard and perfect in its aesthetic content. Don't misunderstand me—I have no time either for those fairies and perverts who spend their whole lives dolling themselves up and putting on make-up, that isn't the kind of care I mean at all. But I believe it is every man's personal duty to himself to keep himself fit and not to waste the perfection of physique the good Lord gave to him at birth. I believe that physical fitness is closely allied to mental sharpness and speed of thought, and I, personally speaking, would never be quick to trust any man who has let his body run to fat."

Johnny Angelo was on a health kick. He took Arthur into his
personal gymnasium and showed him weights and ropes and
horizontal bars. Underneath his flowered silk dressing-gown
he was wearing the tight gold shorts of an athlete. He did
press-ups and trunk-curls, shinned up ropes and pressed,
jerked, held weights until his golden body streamed with
sweat.

He was a new Tarzan, smooth and hairless and golden, with
muscles shimmering right underneath the surface. A pale-
tanned Cassius Clay, the greatest, the prettiest, with white
teeth that smiled smiles of perfect glamour at Arthur. Hanging
upside down, swinging in circles or flat on his back, Johnny
Angelo raised his face and flashed his white and gold smile
without a trace of strain.

"Wrestle with me," said Johnny Angelo. Smiled, white
teeth in his gold tan face. He was too beautiful to be human.

On the mat, tied in knots, Johnny Angelo's big gold body, so
smooth that it slipped through the fingers like water, and
Arthur's pale white body, all blue veins and fragile bones. And
emerging every few seconds like a third contestant, the flash
of white teeth, laughing, dazzling. Because Johnny Angelo
couldn't stop laughing, couldn't stop giggling like a schoolboy.
He got Arthur down and sat full on his belly, holding his
shoulders flat on the canvas and counting slowly up to ten,
choking with laughing. At ten, the count was over, the fight
was through, but Johnny Angelo still sat where he was and
laughed, his eyes wet. Arthur laughed back carefully, not to
commit himself. Eyes into eyes, wet eyes into dry, laughing
eyes into cautious. Arthur's hard eyes went far away, made up
their mind. "Nance," said Arthur.

"What?"

"Fairy."

"What?" said Johnny Angelo. "What are you talking
about?"

"Queer. Keep off me, queer."

"You're crazy. You're out of your mind."

"Not me. You. Lousy fag, keep your hands off me. Nance.
Fairy."

"No," said Johnny Angelo. "No, you must be mad."

Johnny Angelo couldn't believe it. He stared at Arthur
without seeing him. Arthur was backing away from him,
clutching his clothes to his belly, his face red and his mouth

flabby. He kept on blurting out: Queer, Fairy, Fag. A sixteen-year-old bag of bones, pasty and insignificant, who was privileged even to speak to Angelo, to look at him from a distance. And he was calling Johnny Angelo a queer. Not once, but over and over again.

And Johnny Angelo's lips twisted and peeled away from his gums. Disgusted, nauseated. That such filth should come near him, that he should be touched by words like these. He half rose off the mat, meaning to blast Arthur out of existence, destroy him, mash him up into little pieces, but then he stopped and sank back onto his knees again. He was confused. He became dizzy when he moved. And besides, the nausea was too strong, the stench; he didn't want to foul his hands any more. He preferred to keep his distance.

Arthur was red-faced and saucer-eyed. He was like an alarm clock that couldn't shut off. He kept repeating Nance, Fairy, Queer. He stood only a few yards away from Johnny Angelo, the most beautiful, the greatest, the one true hero, and showered him with filth, covering him in slime. Johnny Angelo drew his head in and tried to get up. But he didn't. He couldn't. He had forgotten how to move.

Arthur backed away and then turned his back and ran, out of the gym, out of Johnny's sitting-room and across the front hall, through the front door and away down the street, pulling on loose garments as he went.

Johnny Angelo followed him in a daze. Catsmeat was standing in the hall. "Where is he?" said Johnny Angelo

"Who?"

"Arthur. The boy. Where has he gone?"

"Out," said Catsmeat. "Across the hall and out of the front door and away down the street. What happened?"

"Nothing happened. I want him back."

"Too late to get him back now, he's gone. He'll be halfway home by now."

"Get out and find him," said Angelo. "Don't argue, get right out there and bring him back."

"I can't, it isn't possible. I don't know where he's gone, I don't know where to start. Be reasonable. It just isn't possible "

"It is possible. It must be possible. It can't be not possible."

Catsmeat had never known Johnny Angelo to be so stern and clipped before. it frightened him. So unrhetorical and hard and businesslike.

"What happened?" he asked. "Johnny, tell me what happened."

"Shut up. Nothing happened. I want him found, I want him traced and found before he can do any serious damage."

"Yes," said Catsmeat. "And when I find him?"

"Get rid of him. Do anything you like with him. I mean don't bring him back here again, for fuck's sake. I don't care what you do. But get rid of him. Just get rid of him."

"Yes. And shall I pay him money?"

"No, money isn't safe. We wouldn't ever be sure. Get out, get out there and find him. Get rid of him."

Catsmeat hesitated. He still didn't know what Angelo meant and he was looking carefully into his master's face for signs. He was going slowly and warily, not wanting to make any mistakes.

"Do you mean that?" he said. "Do you really mean that? Get rid of him?"

"Yes, yes," said Angelo, impatient. "That's what I mean. Get rid of him, get him out of my way. Kill him. Wipe him out."

Kill him.

Catsmeat drew in his breath. He was ecstatic and appalled at the same moment. Murder. Real death.

"No kidding," he said. "For real?"

"For real."

Kill him. Have him killed.

"Yes," said Catsmeat. "Just tell me what happened."

"No."

No, Johnny Angelo was telling no one. He'd be embarrassed to disclose anything so trivial and undignified. He sent out Catsmeat and Gattopardo into the streets to find Arthur, and sat alone in his room, thinking things over. And after a minute he began to be sick and he couldn't stop; he vomited himself dry and, when he was empty, he still went on retching helplessly.

Self-hater.

Self-disgust, self-loathing, and it wasn't over yet. Johnny Angelo was out for murder. He was going to wipe out twenty-five years of brawling and plotting and dreaming, two hundred solid pages of non-stop mayhem, triple forte hysteria, all

turned sour on him now, all making him sick. He was going to
kill and obliterate and throw away all the traces. And this was
the end of everything: Kill Arthur. Kill him. Kill it.

25 Death of a Hero

Catsmeat and Gattopardo were gone for half an hour or more.
Johnny Angelo sat where he was and waited. No pacing, no
dramatics. He just sat still and waited.

Catsmeat was standing in the doorway, red-faced, panting.

"Well," said Angelo. "What happened?"

"We got him," Catsmeat said. But he didn't look happy.
"We didn't get on to him right away. We had to go all the way
to the High Street and we thought we'd never catch up with
him. But we saw him. He was standing in the bus queue and
he was crying, but no one was taking any notice, everyone was
pretending they hadn't seen him. And the bus was coming, it
was already drawing in, we didn't have any time to waste and
we couldn't afford to take any chances. So I told Gattopardo to
go ahead. And he took out his gun and shot him."

"Dead?" said Angelo.

"Yes," said Catsmeat. "Dead."

"Yes. And then what?"

"We ran. There wasn't anything else we could do. We could
hardly stand around and talk about the weather. We just
turned round and ran."

"Did anyone follow you?"

"I don't know. We tried to cover our tracks, we tried to
make it tough, that's why we took so long. But I don't know. I
don't know if we made it or not."

"Then," Johnny Angelo said, "we'll just have to wait and
see. We'll just have to hope for the best."

They sat and waited. Catsmeat was crying, and he screamed
every time he heard a car in the street outside. Gattopardo was
standing against the wall, expressionless, mindless, the

zombie. And Angelo was standing by the window and looking out of the window, not moving, not panicking. They waited.

Arthur was already dead. That much Johnny Angelo had already achieved.

They waited. Ten minutes, twenty minutes. No one rang. No police arrived.

But at the end of half an hour the front doorbell rang, and Angelo looked down and the street was full of police cars and sirens. He turned back into the room.

"Yes," he said. "The police."

It was all over. There was no way out, no possible way of escape. Johnny Angelo was caught at last, cornered. He opened a drawer in his desk and took out two silver pistols.

Then took off fast down the back stairs and out of the back door, and he sprinted like hell out into the street, heading left. He had made less than fifteen yards when the first policeman came running round the corner and fired two warning shots above his head, shouting for Johnny Angelo to surrender. There were two choices, give up and get caught and be tried and humiliated and destroyed. Or go on fighting and die quickly in the street.

Die the death of a hero.

He chose. Johnny Angelo faced up to a force of twenty-three armed policemen. He dropped down behind a car. The street was dark and empty.

A grey-haired detective in a brown raincoat stepped forward three paces, cupped his hands around his mouth, and said the things detectives say.

"You can't get away," he said. "Johnny Angelo, we know you're there. Give yourself up."

And Johnny Angelo raised his gun and shot once, bang, very loud and very frightening. The detective stood still and looked at the ground, and then fell over and didn't move.

Twelve policemen attacked him from the front, another ten began an outflanking movement round the back. And Johnny Angelo squatted in cover and watched the glass splinter around him and listened to the sing of the bullets as they flew above him. He was waiting for the end. He was terrified and shaking, but he held back his bullets and saved them, and, when he did raise his gun, he took careful aim and pressed the trigger, bang, bang, and another policeman fell on his knees in the street.

He was shot in the shoulder. He was shot more seriously in the hip-bone, and he deserted his cover, limped away, raced backwards to the better cover of a Bentley parked against a wall. He was shot once in the back, once in the back of his leg, and still he didn't fall. He got behind the cover of the Bentley, with his back against a solid brick wall. He felt safer.

Johnny Angelo. Johnny Angelo. He was shot in the shoulder and the hip-bone, in the back and in his leg, and still he raised his gun and fired. Oh Johnny Angelo, there were policemen dead and dying in the street and Angelo had shot them all.

A bullet dug deep into his flesh, tore deeply just below his heart and he knew at once that he was dead. He fell to his knees behind the car and his blood streamed out from his manywounds and his head whirled and his eyes were blind. He sprawled on the pavement, half kneeling and half lying, and he knew that the police were running forward to bring him in.

But he was the greatest, the greatest, Johnny Angelo was still the greatest. And he rose again, pulled himself back inch by inch onto his feet and staggered out into the open street. He faced his tormentors. Blood was pouring from him, and his life was flowing out with every drop. But he raised his head for one last time and he watched the police as they ran towards him. He pulled his guns, one pistol in his left hand and another in his right, and dying he fired, fired and he fired again, shooting from the hip, his guns blazed flame and the bullets hit home, tore out great lumps of flesh, and bodies fell into the street. One second. Then the police opened fire again. He stood unprotected in the street and they pumped bullets into him; it was an avalanche this time, and they couldn't miss. Johnny Angelo was lifted off his feet and flung backwards. He lay bleeding on the stone. That was an end to it.

No more: his body twitched twice and then he lay still. No more fun for Johnny Angelo.

In death, the greatest. Johnny Angelo was the greatest.

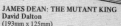

Michael Moorcock

THE RUSSIAN INTELLIGENCE
(193mm x 125mm)

Jerry Cornell is the exact opposite of a super sleuth. Always careful to choose a case that will solve itself so he can spend most of his agency's time in bed with his bird. But his luck runs out when he accidentally takes on the assignment codenamed DEVIL RIDER. The hilarious, detective thriller sequel to *The Chinese Agent*. Illustrated by Harry Douthwaite.

160pp £1.25 Paperback ISBN 0 86130 027 0

SOJAN
(193mm x 125mm)

Moorcock's first Sword & Sorcery hero now in print for the first time in 20 years. The Warrior Lord Sojan battles on a strange and remote planet, his heroic adventures setting the stage for all Moorcock's later champions. The book contains definitive articles by the author on Jerry Cornelius and the secret life of Elric of Melniboné. Illustrated by James Cawthorn.

160pp £0.80 Paperback ISBN 0 86130 000 9

MY EXPERIENCES IN
THE THIRD WORLD WAR . . .
(193mm x 125mm)

The new Savoy Michael Moorcock release for 1980. This original collection of fictional reminiscences, each segment revolving around the interlinking theme of the Third World War, is a powerful emotive work.

176pp £1.50 Paperback ISBN 0 86130 037 8

THE GOLDEN BARGE
(210mm x 148mm)

Pursuing an impossible goal and hounded by dark dreams which drive him to cold-hearted murder, Jephraim Tallow seeks the meaning of life in a wild and intense world. Moorcock's first anti-hero predates the creation of Elric of Melniboné by 12 months in a classic novel that combines the elements of symbolism and fantasy as masterfully as Peake or T. H. White. The high quality, 3-D "Videoback" packaging of this very first Michael Moorcock novel follows Savoy's trendsetting design for *Phoenix Without Ashes* by Harlan Ellison. Illustrated by James Cawthorn.

224pp £1.25 Videoback ISBN 0 86130 002 5

Charles Platt

Who Writes Science Fiction?

(193mm x 125mm)

30 top writers in the field of science fiction tell how they created their most famous books. During a two year period Charles Platt travelled America and England to meet and interview the major names in science fiction that make up this exciting, illuminating and very often surprising book. *Who Writes Science Fiction* is a sequence of interviews, photographs and observations; it is also a very personal and deeply felt book that will undoubtedly be regarded as a seminal work in the genre.

400pp £1.75 Paperback ISBN 0 86130 048 3

- Isaac Asimov
- Thomas M. Disch
- Ben Bova
- Kurt Vonnegut Jr.
- Hank Stine
- Norman Spinrad
- Frederik Pohl
- Samuel R. Delany
- Barry N. Malzberg
- Edward Bryant
- Alfred Bester
- C. M. Kornbluth
- Algis Budrys
- Philip José Farmer
- A. E. Van Vogt
- Philip K. Dick
- Harlan Ellison
- Ray Bradbury
- Frank Herbert
- Damon Knight
- Kate Wilhelm
- Michael Moorcock
- J. G. Ballard
- E. C. Tubb
- Ian Watson
- John Brunner
- Gregory Benford
- Robert Silverberg
- Brian W. Aldiss
- Robert Sheckley

THE GAS
(Introduced by Philip José Farmer)
(193mm x 125mm)

Charles Platt's own classic novel of erotic science fiction is made available for the first time in the UK. It tells the story of a delicious dream that explodes into an uncontrollable nightmare of perversion, violence and insanity; it is also a witty, ironic exposé of the repressions and hypocracies that make us "civilised". (Available only direct from the publisher).

160pp £2.50 Paperback ISBN 0 86130 023 8

SAVOY ANTHOLOGIES

THE SAVOY BOOK
(193mm x 125mm)
The 1970's toughest collection of fiction and graphics.

A superior collection of stories and artwork from the fabulous worlds of science fiction and fantasy: Harlan Ellison, the winner of more science fiction awards than any other writer in history with his brooding story, the prequel to *A Boy and his Dog*; leading English sf writer Brian W Aldiss and Sword & Sorcery master M John Harrison; legendary rock star Jimi Hendrix, who conducts a wild interview from rock 'n' rolls' heaven with Lester Bangs; Paul Buck, Paul Ableman, Michael Butterworth, J Jeff Jones, Heathcote Williams, Richard Kostelanetz, Charles Partington, and artists David Britton, Jim Leon, Bob Jenkins and John Mottershead.

144pp £0.95 Paperback ISBN 0 86130 001 7

THE SAVOY READER
(193mm x 125mm)
Fiction and graphics by William Burroughs, Philip José Farmer, Jack Trevor Story, Jim Leon, Langdon Jones, Heathcote Williams and Gerald Scarfe, as well as Terry Wilson's extensive tributory interview with Brion Gysin, *Planet R101*.

240pp £1.75 Paperback ISBN 0 86130 017 3

NEW WAVE SWORD & SORCERY
(210mm x 148mm)

A breakthrough anthology of general weirdness including Barrington Bailey, M John Harrison, Harlan Ellison, Michael Moorcock and Heathcote Williams. Illustrated in colour and black and white.

224pp £2.50 Paperback ISBN 0 86130 014 9

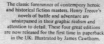